# The Patna Manual of Style

Also by Siddharth Chowdhury

*Day Scholar* (2010)
*Patna Roughcut* (2005)
*Diksha at St. Martin's* (2002)

# The Patna Manual of Style

Stories

SIDDHARTH CHOWDHURY

ALEPH

ALEPH

ALEPH BOOK COMPANY
An independent publishing firm
promoted by ***Rupa Publications India***

Published in India in 2015 by
Aleph Book Company
7/16 Ansari Road, Daryaganj
New Delhi 110 002



This is a work of fiction. Names, characters, places and incidents are either the product of the author's imagination or are used fictitiously and any resemblance to any actual persons, living or dead, events or locales is entirely coincidental.



ISBN: 978-93-83064-77-9

1 3 5 7 9 0 8 6 4 2

Printed and bound in India by Replika Press Pvt. Ltd.

*For*

*Pragya, Sreyash and Tarakeshwari Chowdhury*

# Contents

# The Importer of Blondes}

I remember very clearly the day when I met the redoubtable Jai Shankar Sharma, universally known as Jishnu da, again. It was Christmas Eve of 1998 and at 4.30 in the afternoon I had been fired from my first job. For exactly a week I had been a sub-editor with a third-rung 'lifestyle' magazine called *Touch* which had its offices near Shivaji Stadium in Connaught Place. In that time I contributed four 1,000-word short stories on the lonely theme, starting with 'The Lonely Mother-in-Law'.

The best part of the office, for me, was its location. One could just climb down its dirty mouldy stairs, turn a corner and in a minute was climbing another flight of stairs past a small photo studio and entering Madras Hotel during lunch time and having their fabulous and very reasonably priced masala dosa and filter coffee served in large glass tumblers. After lunch one could go next door to the Central News Agency and browse through their collection of foreign magazines, especially *Granta*, *The New Statesman*, *The New Yorker* and *London Magazine*, which I could ill afford to buy. I had copied the mailing address of *London Magazine* from CNA about a year back when I was still doing my M.Phil and had sent over the next few months two stories about playing cricket in Patna and in return had received one handwritten rejection letter on pale yellow paper from Alan Ross for the second story. He felt I was trying to do too many things in the story and that I should hold back and write simply. I agreed with him. In the end he had written, 'Don't be in a hurry.' Later the following year I would read with much envy in the *London* Magazine 'Tarn Taran', a long excerpt from a forthcoming novel by Anjali Nalwa, an old friend from my undergraduate days at Zakir Husain College, and with whom sadly, I had lost all contact. From CNA one could cross the road and enter the retail outlet of the People's Publishing House in the Outer Circle and buy a lovely Progress Press hardback of Anton Chekhov's *Stories* for the princely sum of eighteen rupees.

About four in the afternoon, the editor of *Touch*, a balding asthmatic sixty-year-old in a starched, white silk kurta-pyjamas topped with a white closed-collar coat with imitation-gold buttons had called me into his cabin smelling of asafoetida which he rubbed on his stomach twice a day for colic and slowly counted thirty-five hundred-rupee notes, put them in a red wedding envelope with a one rupee coin embedded in it and slid it across the off-white sunmica-topped table. Mr Dam shook his head slowly and said to me in his Sylheti dialect, 'The writing game is not for you, try doing something else. Become a gigolo.' Gigolo? I took the money out of the envelope, lit a Gold Flake in his no-smoking office and left. I didn't ask the reason for my sacking because I already knew it, but since he had mystified me with his gigolo remark, I re-entered his office and said to him in return, 'And you will never be an Alan Ross.' At my back I could hear after I slammed the door shut, 'Ross? Ross kay? Kay Ross?' Somehow Mr Dam had got the news that I had taken his private and very confidential secretary Mrs Rifat Kidwai out the other evening. Perhaps one of our sundry pornographer colleagues at the office, like Bukhari the advice column specialist, or Kapoor the illustrator whose specialty was one-forlorn-nipple-peeking-out bodice-rippers, had seen us coming out of the American Centre Library on Kasturba Gandhi Marg where we had gone to see *Casablanca*. Or maybe Berco's where we had gone afterwards for some wonderful Punjabi chop suey paid for by Mrs Kidwai with her new Bobcard. On my devil may care saunter out of Mr Dam's cabin, from where violent coughing could now be heard, I stopped by Mrs Kidwai's desk and kissed the back of her neck softly and before she could react was out in the December chill. A last good kiss. I would miss her sweaty Liril effluvia and generous laughter, not to mention her supremely crisp and flaky keema parathas that she brought wrapped in pink paper napkins from her crumbling haveli in Dariba.

I buttoned up my ancient herringbone, patched up at the elbows and cuffs with scuffed tan leather and lit a fresh Gold Flake from the dwindling embers of the previous one. I like to think that Connaught Place in December is like Paris in the springtime. You can't be unhappy there for long. Not that I have ever been to Paris, only admired the wide boulevards, the Citroëns and the leisurely street-side cafes with their marble-top tables from afar, in countless Truffaut and Godard movies. Not to mention my absolute favourite, Jean-Pierre Melville, whose poster of *Le Samouraï* with Alain Delon looking ice-cold in a Burberry trench coat, bought by my father from College Street in Calcutta, perhaps still adorns a wall in my bedroom in Patna.

But it is not the eternally sunny Maurice Chevalier I hear, singing about little girls with winning smiles but good old Miles blowing his trumpet while I take a detour through Central Park and stop to buy some roasted peanuts. More often than not it is 'My Funny Valentine'.

In exactly five minutes my disappointment at the fatal loss of my job was over and as I rustled the new, crisp Bank of Baroda notes in my jacket pocket, I started feeling positively buoyant. I was good for the month, the rent at the hotel was paid and I only had to pay around five hundred rupees to the dhaba owner in Chuna Mandi where I had my dinner of thick rajma curry, dal fry and four tandoori rotis greased with Amul butter. So that left me about three thousand rupees to play around with. It was the most amount of money I'd had with me in one go for a long time. In my khaki canvas satchel I also had a cheque for rupees three hundred and fifty from a Hindi daily for a Cortázar translation I had done for their Sunday supplement. For a couple of weeks I could work on my novel and then, look for another job. Flush with all this money I decided to have a long overdue shave at a saloon in Shankar Market and later have the Patna Large at Yadavji Litti Centre in one of the by-lanes leading to the New Delhi Railway Station on the Paharganj side. The Patna Large was four litties, two pieces of mutton in fiery red gravy, brinjal and potato chokha and a small katori of desi ghee. All this life-affirming fare for rupees twenty only. The clientele was mostly auto and taxi drivers along with Paharganj coolies in their red tunics. After a dose of Patna Large all the burden of the world felt as light as a raindrop on an upturned face. The day before I had noticed the first two strands of silvery grey in my beard. As I watched the barber lather my face with V-John shaving cream, skillfully trim and then shave the beard off, I felt a twinge of regret. The beard had been my companion for the better part of the year, as I had struggled with my novel. The novel, about my first year at Delhi University in a student's lodge called Shokeen Niwas, was already eight-hundred pages long and I had not even reached Winter term. Now with a new face I felt I could start afresh.

With the beard gone and a thick moustache in place I looked more grown-up and purposeful, which I felt was a good thing and at the age of twenty-three quite welcome. The steamed white napkin felt good against my skin and made me comfortably drowsy. I felt like slipping into an early morning dream in my house in Kadam Kuan, Patna which I had not visited in close to a year. That I didn't finish my course work in my M.Phil in Shakespeare Studies was a huge disappointment to my parents. The fact that I had moved out of my hostel room at Gwyer Hall and the university and was now living in a rathole called Kama in Paharganj didn't endear me much either. I rarely called them up anymore as I had nothing to say and they didn't have my number. One of the hardest things in this world is to reconcile with the disappointment that you sense in your parents' voices even when they are trying to be helpful. You can feel their acute suffering as they reach out to you but can't. They are all at sea. You just have to put the receiver down and close your eyes and gently rest your head against the glass pane of the telephone booth then.

I had got the job at *Touch* through Ritwik Ray, a short-story writer I admired in Patna, after I had called him very early one morning, when the phone rates were cheaper, drunk, despondent and broke, a couple of weeks back. He asked me to meet Dam Sahab, who in his youth had published a left-wing poetry journal from Patna and whom Ritwik knew from his Patna cine-society days. For many of us young writers in

Patna and Delhi in the 1990s, Ritwik Ray was someone we all looked up to. His novellas and slim anthology of stories like *The Prince of Patna*; *The Crown Jewels*; *Harry da and Other Stories*; *Mao for the Misbegotten* were passed from one literary acolyte to another like talismans. It was the Masonic handshake that guaranteed lifelong friendships. From his stories we learnt about socialism and how to use it while writing political fiction, this side of polemic. He was our own private Cortázar, our Trumbo, our Zaheer 'Zed' Abdali, our Kashinath Singh. His was the shining path we wished to traverse. We copied his look, noticed his style (or the lack of it), the full Hemingway beard with its flecks of premature grey, the thick reversible Khadi Gram Udyog Bhavan bundi over the regulation white shirt and denims in winter, the police surplus store khaki satchel and the gleaming black Yezdi, his pride and joy, on the back seat of which sat the latest prototype of Mira Varma, his great lost love: dusky, in Cottage Emporium saris, kohl-lined eyes concealed by Ray-Ban Wayfarers, troubled and aloof. I had borrowed the Yezdi when my own great love Charulata Roy had come to Patna from Dhanbad to take her National Eligibility Test (NET) for lectureship last year and we had driven out to the Gandhi Setu bridge which connected Patna to north Bihar and watched the barges sail majestically towards Benares on the preternaturally calm Ganges in the twilight.

Fiction for Ritwik was only a tool for class struggle. It was to be used forever against the rich, the middle classes and in the defence of the poor, the marginalized. Even though I agreed entirely with him, I neither had his strength of conviction nor his streak of uncompromising austerity. I was forever in doubt and, moreover, poverty didn't agree with me.

'Take the job if he offers you one. Even though I must warn you that the magazine he publishes is just about rubbish. Work on your novel. That is the most important thing. Besides money is always welcome. Just hang in there till I set you up with something in publishing soon.' Ritwik's voice, as calm and warm-hearted as ever, even though it was just before five and he had a quarter-bottle-of-Old Monk-a-night habit. An aristocrat by birth and a Marxist by conviction, Ritwik knew the terrible despondency that could afflict a writer of fiction, having experienced it many times himself, and that a little compassion went a long way. In a day or two everything would be fine. God bless him.

Just then I felt a gentle tap on my shoulder, turned and saw Jishnu da looking at me with his thin emaciated village purohit of a face. A face at once sly and privileged, used to the daily extraction of petty money. The Gandhi glasses still gave him a scholarly look. There was a clear division down the middle of his face. The left side was droopy and shut down and the right one alert and sharp. It was the right one I remembered from my days at Shokeen Niwas, the students' lodge on Bungalow Road run by our legendary landlord Zorawar Singh Shokeen, where I had stayed the first year of my time in Delhi University. I still remember the feral glint in his eyes as he slashed my wrist with an astura as he believed that I had betrayed him and Zorawar over a girl, close to half a decade back. I had left Shokeen Niwas soon after. Zorawar Singh Shokeen was now a ward councillor from Nangia Park. Though Jishnu da had expressed remorse to many of our friends, I had not kept in touch with him. As he embraced me heartily the only thought in my mind was—if only I had not been hasty in shaving off my beard, Jishnu da would have passed the barber shop without recognizing me and my day would have been different. Of all the saloons in the world, he of course had to walk into mine.

'Six years, you and Pranjal never came to visit me after you left Shokeen Niwas.' Pranjal was my roommate and best friend. Over the years I had lost touch with him too. More and more, as I worked on my novel, it made me cold and self-contained. Friends noticed and stayed away.

'We heard that you had moved out of Shokeen Niwas.'

'Not true, Hriday babu, you didn't meet me because you thought I was a bastard and I didn't meet you because I realized you were right. Here, we will make things even—close all accounts. Today is a historic day,' Jishnu da said dramatically and took the astura from the barber, who looked on with a vacant smile. 'Here, take this and cut me open too.' Jishnu da put the astura in my hand and rubbed it near his left wrist.

'Don't act like an idiot, Jishnu da, we have no accounts to reconcile, I forgave you a long time back.'

'No, you didn't. All right, hit me in the face. I have thought about this moment for five, no, six years. You must forgive me. Cut me up, hit me, beat me to a pulp.' Jishnu da was working himself up to his usual frenzy of passion before war. The barber was not smiling anymore. Like any normal god-fearing man he too actively realized that here was a man whose will was stronger than most and it was better to get out of the way and not antagonize him further. Since I knew that this dramatic monologue would go on for some time till I either embraced him back heartily or actually cut him with the astura, I chose to do the next best thing. I hit him with a backhand cross court slap which sent him sprawling out of the saloon. I could write a short story about the expression on Jishnu da's face as I picked him up outside the saloon. To cut a long story short, I can tell you he was not expecting the slap. He was sure it would be an embrace. It is always an embrace. I gave a twenty-rupee note to the barber and didn't wait for the change. It was, I guess, a day ordained for grand gestures.

Even though a part of my brain told me to be on guard so that I didn't get shot in the back by Jishnu da, the other part of my brain was processing the long forgotten thrill of his company, his waywardness, the illicit unpredictableness of his life. By this time we were back in the Outer Circle walking towards Volga where he wanted to catch the happy hours before they ended at six. Jishnu da took out a ganja-filled Navy Cut from the side pocket of the olive corduroy jacket that he was wearing and lit it. After taking a long lung-withering drag, he passed the roach along to me and recited softly a few lines from our national poet Ramdhari Singh Dinkar's cult-classic 'Shakti aur Kshama'. Power and Forgiveness. Lines which are carved in high relief on the memory of every Bihari schoolboy and girl of a certain vintage who like me has declaimed it full of veer-ras from the proscenium of the school auditorium on Annual Day.

*Kshama shobhti us bhujang ko*
*Jiske paas garal ho*
*Usko kya jo dantheen,*
*Vishrahit, vineet, saral ho.*

A free translation would go somewhat like this:
Absolution, mind you, is the privilege
Only of the truly venomous serpent
And not of one which is de-fanged
Non-venomous, naive, and servile to boot.

My grandmother had once heard Ramdhari Singh Dinkar recite that iconic poem at Darbhanga House, and was smitten for life like so many Patna women of that time. 'My god, the complexion, the complexion,' she would always sigh at the end of her narrative which to my mind invariably would bring back the image of Marlon Brando whispering 'the horror, the horror' at the end of *Apocalypse Now*. Dinkarji, God bless his immortal soul, set the tone for the evening.

Small greyish-blue clouds were gathering over the horizon and I could hear a distant thunderclap over the Qutub Minar. I had heard that morning on the ancient Telerama TV, kept at the hotel reception counter, that there had been a sprinkling of light rain in Patna yesterday. A phenomenon which Doordarshan weather forecasters in the 1980s would term regularly as *garaj ke saath chheente*, a phrase that would invariably bring to mind some especially dreadful manifestation of Irritable Bowel Syndrome. A condition which as a Brahmin I was more than aware of. When it comes to the weather Delhi and Patna are like conjoined twins. When it rains in Patna, Delhi will invariably conjure up a thunderstorm the very next day. It is the extremes of emotion when it comes to the climate I like about both places. In the summer you can feel the heat seep into your blood and keep it on a slow simmer, and in the winter chill it to a happy slowness. And when it rains, it merrily mixes with your blood and makes you lighter. In both the places you can't be indifferent to the elemental. Whether it be the storm lashing Mehrauli or the one raging in your heart.

'Hriday, what do you do now? Are you working? Or still writing Manohar Kahaniyan?' Jishnu da asked me, rubbing his cheek pointedly.

I laughed and said, 'Yes, I am writing still. Trying to write a novel.'

Jishnu da slapped me on the back and said with much pleasure, 'You were always very odd. Writing a novel! Always said you would. What is your novel about?'

'It is a violent love story.'

'Is it about me?' Jishnu da laughed some more. With each peal of laughter I was getting a bit more reassured that he might not knife me in the back yet. But then with someone like Jishnu da you couldn't ever be fully certain.

'No.'

'You should write about me. I am quite a character,' Jishnu da said casually, a bemused smile on his face, eyes looking up at the Statesman House building. Heroic gaze into fading light.

'Perhaps someday I will. If I live long enough.'

As we entered the dark, smoke-filled Volga I asked Jishnu da, 'What do you do now? I am quite surprised that you are still alive, boss.' As we sat at the corner-most table in the half empty restaurant, Jishnu da said to me, 'I am an Importer of Blondes.'

Then over a pitcher of draught beer and a large bowl of peanuts mixed with green chillies and onion, Jishnu da narrated to me his violent love story.

Three years back he started as an assistant to a big time Punjabi event manager called Rajbir Jindal whom he knew from his university days when they had worked for the Congress and the BJP alternatively each year and sometimes both in the same year. Rajbir's father, a well-known tent-wallah, was a friend of our landlord Zorawar Singh Shokeen.

'This is the same Rajbir, whose sister Prachi you used to screw during our first year?'

'The very same. You have a good memory, Hriday. But then you always did, when it came to women.' Prachi Jindal had been a presidential candidate in the university elections that year and I along with all of our Shokeen Niwas hostelmates had campaigned for her extensively.

Soda Lemon

Ginger pop

Prachi Jindal

On the Top

She won of course. Due to a last-minute sympathy wave after someone shot at her car in Hudson Lines near North Campus and shattered the windscreen.

Rajbir Jindal on the other hand had once won a councillor's seat on an ABVP ticket but when in the following years they didn't nominate him for president switched to the NSUI. But the NSUI too denied him a ticket and he fought independently and came third with 5,000 votes, behind the ABVP and the NSUI. Rajbir obviously didn't have his sister's luck, even though Jishnu da had helped him in his campaign too. But those 5,000 votes, apart from the fact that he was Prachi Jindal's brother, gave him a 'standing' in Delhi University politics. A status which also came in handy when a few years later he opened an event management company after he fell out with his father. So after Jishnu da had exhausted all his four attempts at the Civil Services, he joined Jindal in his event management business. From weddings to shraddha, chautha, uthala to product launches to book readings, they organized anything that needed to be organized and in cash-rich, newly liberalized Delhi, there was no dearth of events to manage. In recent times, in Delhi, a lot of Biharis had joined the event management bandwagon and most of them, judging by the spanking new white Maruti Suzuki Gypsies parked in the lanes of North Campus colonies, were doing rather well for themselves.

'Do you know why we Biharis do so well in this business?'

I dutifully shook my head, not that Jishnu da noticed.

'That is because we can manage anything. Nothing fazes us. We have infinite patience and our skin is made of stainless steel. Scratch-proof. When we are standing in a queue, we are not thinking of air conditioners. We are the most philosophical of Indians and of course this is the only way we can make friends. Everybody and their dadi has a Bihari friend who manages to get a ration card to a gas connection to a passport for them. We make for good true friends. Resourceful ones. We are that very extinct commodity now, that never-do-well younger chacha or cousin who was earlier found in all middle-class homes and was indispensable to all social occasions and oddball jobs. Nowadays everybody works. Nobody is unemployed. And that is where we come in, the Bihari friend who will manage everything for you. And let me tell you, people pay good money to anyone who will offer to carry the burden of their worries for them. In these modern times, a Bihari friend is worth his weight in gold. And if you are not lucky you can always call Jishnu Sharma, only he costs a bit extra.'

Even his tone and enunciation now had that exaggerated Patna lilt, a lilt that made you run your fingers delicately through your hair while you spoke, and which Delhi somehow couldn't seem to get enough of, ever since the great Bihari linguist Laloo Prasad Yadav had arrived on the scene. Jishnu da had decided to do dukandari on his Patna legacy. And why not.

From managing marriages, soon Jindal and Jishnu da graduated to managing dance troupes. The girls in these troupes were usually ersatz belly dancers from the breakaway Soviet Republics—Ukraine, Georgia, Kazakhstan, Uzbekistan and also from the Balkans, especially Estonia and bordering Belarus. These girls would descend on Delhi around October and stay till March. They would be booked in advance by Jindal and Jishnu da for performances at all two-and three-star hotels in Delhi and the upcoming satellite towns of Gurgaon and Noida. Also, the girls would be booked for private parties: bachelor nights, birthdays, Diwali, Christmas and New Year parties in farm houses. A one-hour dance performance and an hour of mingling with the guests at a private party usually cost around Rs 2,50,000 for five girls and in hotels the rate was double. The more number of hours the girl could clock, the more money they would earn. Jishnu da also employed a Palestinian DJ-cum-synthesizer player called Mourad who had originally come to study dentistry and a Nigerian drummer named Maurice, who were paid by the week during the season. They named their new venture The Footfall Dance Company.

After Jishnu da asked the waiter for a refill, he pulled out a small 4×7 pink-and-gold wedding album from his jacket pocket and propped it open on the table. In it were his fabled blondes. There were about ten girls in all. Two photographs each. One a regular portrait and the other in a belly-dancing costume. My maternal uncle had been a medical officer at the Bokaro Steel Plant when it was still being run by Russians in the sixties. There he had forged friendships, which continued for generations, as later his sons too went off to Leningrad to study medicine. From her brother my mother had developed the taste for Russian lemon tea, which I too enjoyed with my Turgenev in the afternoon after lunch. Till 1990 we would also regularly receive at our house in Patna every month a slim, folded brown paper-wrapped copy of *Soviet Woman* magazine in the mail. In it I would learn of the innate resilience of Russian women and their expertise in handling large farm equipments and at raucous dancing wearing colourful costumes amidst freshly cut stacks of barley.

I picked up the album and flipped slowly through it with Jishnu da providing a running commentary: 'ah that is Rukhsana, she is from Farghana, same place as Babur, could be related even. That's Svetlana Vorsin, our showstopper, I call her Shweta. She is from Minsk.' And so on. The girls were all extraordinarily pretty and quite young. All between seventeen to twenty-five years of age. And then I paused at the last photograph in the album. The headshot was there, but the corresponding belly-dancing snap had been removed. The impression of the absent photograph was still there on the thin plastic foil of the album.

The sloe eyes bluer than the Danube, this was simply the prettiest girl I had ever seen. 'And this, Hriday Babu, is the love of my life. Anna Kuchma from Odessa.' Anna was the fourth of five daughters of a never-do-well plumber who at dot 9 a.m. each morning started drinking vodka mixed with grapefruit juice whom people called for work at their own peril. Because he was so mild-natured, Boris Kuchma, in spite of his drinking got regular work, though he was liable to change the whole kitchen sink when you only wanted him to look at the washer. Even though the family never had much money, it was not unduly an unhappy one. The mother Helena looked after the kids as well as she could and supplemented the family income with her job as a beautician. As time went on it was Helena's money rather than Boris's increasingly patchy income that the family subsisted on. And then one day in the morning as Anna prepared to leave for her school, she found Boris slumped on the sofa with his right hand stretched towards the Stolichnaya bottle kept on a table beside the sofa, a smile of anticipation on his face. He was dead of a massive coronary stroke. The TV was on and replaying scenes of the Berlin Wall coming down, brick by each hand-plucked brick. Things changed for the family thereafter. 'The role of the patriarch is very important, Hriday. Even though he may be an ineffectual one, his presence alone keeps the family together. The fact that Father would be home was enough deterrent for me not to drink beer in Patna. Though he hardly would have noticed. He had, as you know, great expectations from me. He wanted to see me ride into Patna in a white Ambassador car with a red beacon light on top and all sirens blaring. I failed him miserably. He does not speak to me anymore. But the fact that he is there in Patna, every morning going to the Gandhi Maidan for his walk in his Khadi Gram Udyog Bhavan kurta and dhoti, is enough for me. When I feel unhappy I always think of that and it cheers me up. He was a friend of Rahulji when he was in the Kisan Sabha. I too come from a family of scholars. Volga se Ganga tak.' He giggled and raised his glass in toast to the great Rahul Sankritayana. It was a revelation to me that even Jishnu da, an intrepid positive thinker who perhaps never had a doubt in his life, could feel profound unhappiness at times.

So basically after Boris Kuchma died the family started

breaking up. Anyway the two older sisters were married and lived with their husbands in Kiev. They had married a pair of brothers who were bricklayers. The one just older than Anna joined the Church and soon after Anna dropped out of school. She was thirteen years old. Helena, the mother, too, within a year of Boris's death married an electrician and moved to Kiev with Anna and Maria, the youngest. But one afternoon after her stepfather kissed her behind the wood shed and tried to open her blouse, Anna left home that very evening never to return.

By this time the waiter who was dressed as Santa Claus had brought a third pitcher of beer and started pouring it in our glasses. The beer with the ganja had produced a nice mellow feeling in me and I had even started feeling nostalgic about Jishnu da and our friendship from the Shokeen Niwas days. Also the storyteller's intrinsic hunger for new material had taken over.

'So what happened to Anna Kuchma? How did she survive? What did she do?' I asked Jishnu da.

'Well, the facts are not very clear and she herself has told me a couple of versions, but somehow she reached Minsk, hitchhiking all the way and there she joined the Belarus Circus Company as an apprentice belly dancer. She performed the dance of the seven veils under the stage name of Nigar Afsana. A name given to her by the Tajik lion-tamer Kemal, an inveterate Bollywood filmchi, whose one passion in life was to meet Mithun Chakraborty and sing "I Am A Disco-dancer" with him. He even had the shiny silver-white jumpsuit, which doubled as his lion-taming poshak. The wages were wretched but at meal times the potatoes were plentiful and Anna got to share a dormitory-style tent with six other girls. One of the girls sharing the tent with her was Svetlana Vorsin, yes, the blonde Shweta from Minsk. She was about eighteen then, a couple of years older than Anna. They struck up a close friendship. Svetlana was a trapeze artist and has the most flexible body I have ever seen on a girl. Here's a little detail. She can do the doggie style just balanced on her two hands on the floor. No knees, baby. It is like Wonder Woman in mid-flight. You do not even need Afghan Snow. Amazing muscle control.'

I finished my glass of beer in a single gulp and poured some more from the pitcher. The only thought in my mind was 'Afghan Snow!' Surely Pond's Cold Cream would be more appropriate but I guess nothing but the best for Jishnu da. So Afghan Snow it is. Jishnu da carried on with his narrative.

'The Belarus Circus Company was run by an enterprising middle-aged strongman called Sandow Martynov. Martynov's single specialty was that in the middle of the show he would come out to the centre of the circus area dressed as an Indian Maharaja, faux diadem and peacock feather, leading a column of three fearsome Indian elephants which he had bought from a temple in Alleppey. The elephants were named Ganga, Jamuna and Saraswati, would you believe it. Martynov would lie down and one by one Ganga, Jamuna and in the end the mythical Saraswati, would walk across his body after stepping on his chest to thunderous applause from the audience. Usually there would be an encore. Martynov's other specialty was girls. He really loved them but Anna was safe from him as he preferred them quite young. By the time girls turned thirteen, you know when they start to bleed, he usually lost all interest in them. He also ran an orphanage in Minsk from where he had a steady supply. Many of the girls when they grew up became part of the troupe and performed as showgirls and trapeze artists. Svetlana was one of the alumnae of the Martynov Orphanage. And when six months back one eleven-year-old Uzbek girl put a knitting needle through Martynov's left eye, pushing it all the way to his medulla oblongata, Svetlana ordered champagne all around, sitting right at this table and we drank through the night.'

So Anna and Svetlana became good friends and a year later when the Belarus Circus Company was touring Sweden they decided to jump ship at Stockholm and strike out on their own. Both of them got work as waitresses at a strip joint and in a few months' time both had Swedish passports.

'I will arise and go now and go to Innisfree.' I arose and looked for a large pot to piss in.

Jishnu da asked the waiter to bring two large whiskies while I walked to the toilet on largely unsteady legs. I had not drunk so much in months because of self-imposed austerity measures. I wished that Jishnu da would order some food to soak the alcohol, a kebab platter, a full Chicken Taliban, but no such luck. I was famished. Those days I constantly thought about food, I was hungry all the time. The months of relentless rajma-roti had taken their toll.

The time was close to eight now. When I returned from Innisfree I saw Jishnu da had finished half of his whisky and was looking balefully towards two young backpackers who were sitting at the next table. From their accent and snatches of conversation I could gather they were from Israel. The boy's unshaven face and long hair and the girl's tie-dyed pyjamas and Rajneesh prayer beads couldn't hide the alert military training they had undergone. In a few months' time they would be back at their posts on the Gaza Strip, freshly scrubbed and in military fatigues. It is said that the Indian Jews, Baghdadi from Calcutta, Bene Israel from Maharashtra and Cochini from Kerala, saw prejudice based on colour and race for the first time when they migrated to Israel, the Promised Land, dominated as the society was by white European Ashkenazi Jews who had survived the Holocaust by the skin of their teeth.

I sipped my large Peter Scot slowly. We had been drinking steadily for the past two hours. Jishnu da was staring at the Israeli couple quite blatantly now. To divert his attention and to hurry his story along I asked him, 'So, Jishnu da, don't tell me you met Anna Kuchma in Sweden?'

'No, I didn't. I met her and Svetlana in London. With Jindal, the previous year. We were auditioning girls for an "arthouse" movie at a nightclub in Chinatown, off Gerard Street. And in walked Svetlana Vorsin. She was lovely in a black turtleneck and blue jeans, without an ounce of make-up on, which as you might know is absolutely unheard of in London. We had been auditioning girls all afternoon but as soon as we told them what we wanted they would leave. Well, how to say it, they had no artistic integrity. So when the first thing that Svetlana says when Jindal throws her the pitch is "you want to do a fuck movie, yes?" we knew we had finally struck gold.

'We paid her two thousand pounds in cash for two days and shot five movies in a house in East Hounslow. One hour each. We did the whole diaspora experience. Indian boys doing blonde girls. What could be better than that?

'*Phagwara da Lund* in Punjabi, *Inglistani Chut* in Hindi, *Patel Rape* in Gujarati, *Dirty Be Harry* in Bhojpuri and my favourite dedicated to you and all my Bengali friends,

*Bokachoda in London*. In fact I liked *Bokachoda* so much that I wanted to do a whole series. *Bokachoda in LA*, *Bokachoda in Paris* but Jindal backed out. But it is still an idea. I am a born connoisseur of Bengali culture, having fucked so many of them over the years . . . Maybe one day I will do it on my own. I wrote all five screenplays. I remember you used to write in the early morning light in Shokeen Niwas. Some of that discipline must have rubbed off on me. I loved directing too. My specialty is monumental close-ups. A single red nipple, protuberant like a cherry, the dilated eyes, to say nothing of the anus, a lingering shot of the shaved and petalled chut and then the cum shot at 24 frames per second, set to remixed music from Manoj Kumar classics, especially *Purab aur Paschim. Hai Preet Jahan Ki Reet Sada/Main Geet Wahin Ke Gata Hoon. Bharat Ka Rehnewala Hoon/Bharat Ki Baat Sunata Hoon*. I am the talent. Jindal is only the money.'

'Well, Jishnu da, you are a regular Peckinpah. Also when you do *Bokachoda in Paris*, can I please play the lead? Have always wanted to see Paris. We can shoot on the Left Bank. Near La Closerie des Lilas. It is a clean well-lighted place I hear.'

As Santa Claus refreshed our glasses, Jishnu da went back to staring at the Israeli girl. So I sipped my whisky, lit the mandatory Gold Flake and asked him, 'But Anna?'

'Patience, Hriday, patience. I was coming to that. Anna came for the wrap party with our Shweta.'

'You had a wrap party for a porn movie?'

'Sure. The crew wanted it. The crew was British, you see. You have to do these things. You know, do in Patna as the Yadavs do. *Rome me Pope and Patna me Gope*. All that kind of thing. And anyway I am always game for a party, am

I not? Jindal didn't want to but I made him cough up the money. The stingy tent-wallah.' It was it seems love at first sight for Jishnu da when he met Anna at the wrap party. Anna was quieter and more self-contained than Svetlana. Whereas Svetlana was the enterprising, bubbly go-getter, who was all for a wild night of partying, Anna would rather stay at home and read Japanese comic books. 'One thing, though, in the evenings Anna likes to swim so I would take her out to the YMCA pool on Jai Singh Road and there she would do her ten laps and would be as happy as a Labrador pup afterwards. It would be at the swimming pool that I would hear her laugh for the first time. Before that it was only a meagre smile I had seen her manage once in a while and that too only when Svetlana would playfully tickle her neck from behind. She is apparently very ticklish.'

When Jindal made a suggestion to Svetlana about putting together a troupe of belly dancers to tour India, Svetlana was all for it and she persuaded Anna to come with her. Not that it needed much of a persuasion, Anna always followed Svetlana in whatever she did. According to Jishnu da Anna and Svetlana seemed to be two sides of the same coin. One side frayed and rubbed out, the other glinting in the sunlight. They did everything together, shared the same clothes, did each other's make-up, shampooed each other's hair and ate off the same plate, Muslim style.

'When I look at Anna, I feel a cloak of infinite calmness descend over me. I take in her fingers, slender and long, and watch them run through Svetlana's hair, brushing it back to make a schoolgirl ponytail and I want to kiss the tips of her fingers and wish my hair were long too. I watch her sip her talumein soup at Berco's, each spoonful a study in grace, and

I want to dab the corners of her lips after each swallow and lean over and kiss them before the next spoonful. Somehow I suppress this urgent need and not make a fool of myself. In the mornings I watch her do her padmasana aglow in the winter sun and see the sweat spread across the bottom of her ratty Lonsdale sweatpants. I want to peel them off her legs and wear them myself. We are the same size. Sometimes I take her sweatpants off the floor in her room and take them into my own and wash them in Genteel with my own clothes. She notices I am sure but does not say anything. To be of constant help to her is my only desire. On Sunday mornings, while regular folk laze around and read the thick and colourful newspaper supplements, I like to polish my two pairs of calf-leather riding boots, custom-made by a one-armed Chinese shoemaker in Macau. One reddish brown, the other black. You don't need an actual horse to wear riding boots, only the temperament. I use a soft-cloth to evenly apply the polish all over and then leave the boots to soak it through for twenty minutes and then with two pairs of brushes buff it to perfection. One brush pushing with the grain, the other against. Just like in a marriage. Anna on those days comes into my room quietly and puts her reddish brown all-weather walking shoes beside my boots and tiptoes away. This is how she shows her fondness, how much she trusts me. I for one wouldn't let anyone touch my boots.' Here Jishnu da shot a challenging look at Santa Claus, then leaned back and put his right leg on the table and pulled back his jeans so that I could admire his gleaming black boots. They were truly magnificent. If only Jishnu da had granted the shoemaker two hands instead of the measly one these surely would have been the Taj Mahal of boots.

Though Jishnu da had fallen, as they say, head over heels in love with her, the reverse lamentably was not true. 'You know, Hriday, Anna just made me a better man than I was. When I am with her there is no stress, there is no need to play games, screw someone, slap someone if he has grazed your car, like it is in Delhi all the time. When I am with Anna, I am almost the son my father wanted to have.' The last statement I doubted very much but didn't say anything. Even though Anna was not in love with Jishnu da, he was the only one she would talk to, in her broken English. She didn't trust Jindal from the start. Through long weeks of travelling and performing in various Indian cities she would narrate to Jishnu da all about her life and the fascinating journey of her young life. 'It was enough for me. Just to sit next to her on the plane or in hotel lounges between the shows and listen to her. I didn't want anything else. Well, not entirely true. I wanted to make love to her all day, all night but only when she would let me. I have had many women. I like women as you know. It is one of my indulgences, I do not deny it. But I am not a raper, not even in my dreams, and besides Anna was different. I was prepared to wait, she trusted me and could perhaps sense I was in love with her. Women sense these things more quickly than us. If there was ever any trouble it was me she would call to sort things out. Here in Connaught Place, after a show at the Marina Hotel, just around the corner, a couple of inebriated Punjabis, Chaddha-Chawlas, Tusi-Mainus, somehow reached her room and started banging on the door. She called me on my mobile phone. I came out and literally broke them with my bare hands. *Khopdi khol diye*. On the other hand Jindal and Svetlana had grown closer. By the second month of our tour Jindal and Svetlana were sharing the same room. I had no illusions about Svetlana. She was like a heat-seeking missile when it came to money. And Jindal was the money. The Footfall Dance Company was doing well. We were booked from here to forever. Anna was our star. True to her stage name, Nigar Afsana, she was a born storyteller under the lights. All her quietness, the awkwardness, the withdrawn shyness would disappear and in its place there would be sensuality, grace, a troubled edge air to her dance, which left the audience mesmerized. Where with the other girls with their mechanical full-on posturing, the audience would get on their feet dancing and try to climb the stage, with Anna it was like she were telling each one of them their own love story. She could get into the memory of the audience. Her favourite number was the one I selected for her. It is from that old Hindi movie of our childhood, *Ghulami*, with Mithun Chakraborty and Anita Raaj, 'Zihale Masti'. Every time she performs that number, I feel as if she were speaking only to me. *Tumhare Seene Se Uthta Dhuan, Hamare Dil Se Guzar Raha Hai*. The wisp of blue smoke, full of longing, out of your heart is passing through mine.

The Israeli girl, Ashkenazi and blonde, was holding her partner's head gently with both hands, elbows on the table. She whispered something to the boy and he turned and looked at us, smiling. I gave him a thumbs-up sign and lit a Gold Flake. This fond holding of the head of the lover brought to my mind memories of my own Charulata Roy, who, tired of waiting for me to do something worthwhile, had finally married the boy her parents had selected for her. We had been together since our university days. That was the night I had called up Ritwik at 3 a.m., after failing to reach Charulata after many attempts. It hadn't yet sunk in fully that

I had lost Charulata forever and wouldn't ever see her again, that she would never run her fingers through my hair again. It had only been a month since her marriage but under the circumstances I was bearing up quite well. If only I could keep working on my novel, I would be all right. And at the back of my mind was the possibility that Charu would soon realize her folly and return to me. My optimism was such.

Jishnu da lit a Gold Flake and then continued, 'I never thought I would fall in love with a Western girl. The white skin does not hold any fascination for me. I like fair Indian skin, Brahmin skin, with a hint of pink around the nipples, not the leprous white, and I have never understood this craze for blondes. One of the things which made us survive the British was the utter contempt with which they were regarded by us Brahmins. We wouldn't even drink water in their homes, nor offer them any if they came to ours. This withering life-affirming contempt made us endure every depredation of the British, like it did of the Muslims before. Prejudice kept us sane. We were better than them and if we didn't notice them or acknowledge them, they would go away and they did. All those censuses, all those caste surveys, gazetteers of sterling clerkship, meant to divide the Hindu nation but to no avail. In the end they had to leave. As if facts alone could explain India. All this was drilled into me when I was a child, by my father, one of his ancestors died fighting the British alongside Kuer Singh in 1857. You Bengalis came fifty years later to the fight, we Biharis were there first. When I go to London, by the third day I start to get claustrophobic walking the streets. I start to hyperventilate. These people ruled us for 200 years. How the fuck did that happen? The rage and shame I feel is all-consuming. I have to get out then. Why do you write in English? Write in Hindi from now on. That's your bloody rashtrabhasha, or have you forgotten it? And then one day Anna Kuchma arrives and I forget everything. That she is a firang, Christian, daughter of a plumber and I am a Brahmin, Saryuparin from head to toe. Everything seems irrelevant and I wish to start anew. I will do dharm-parivartan and call myself Johnny. Though probably in Patna they will continue to call me Bhadwa Sharma. This janeu is not made of cotton but copper. It is cutting into my skin. One of these days I am going to get a wire-cutter and rip it off.' Jishnu da finished his glass of Peter Scot in a desperate gulp, balanced it delicately on his head and signalled Santa Claus to recharge it. He then put his yellowed janeu inside his denim shirt which in his excitement he had taken out to prove his point and recited in an undertone:

*Duryodhan woh bhi de na saka*
*Ashish samaj ki le na saka*

Oh dear, Dinkar again.

'It seems, Jishnu da, that you have finally attained nirvana. Can we order some kebabs?'

'I have,' he accepted gravely but said nothing about the kebabs.

So, as the fortunes of the Footfall Dance Company soared, the two partners Jishnu da and Jindal were hopelessly in love with their leading dancers. One requited and the other wholly unrequited. The surprise element was how Jindal, a hard-bitten, crocodile-skinned, out and out Delhi punter for whom women were no better than a post-four pegs at midnight diversion, was smitten by this Belarusian minx. Even though Jindal held on to the purse strings, it was Svetlana who actually called the shots in the hiring and firing of girls, selecting the venues and, increasingly, negotiating with hotels and private clients. Svetlana, when Jindal was away visiting his wife and children, was not averse to balling Jishnu da on the side a couple of times but they were discreet about it. 'It was just a biological need. We were good together. She knew I was Jindal's right-hand man and I knew she was Jindal's girl and that was fine. I don't think she was in love with Jindal at all. On the other hand I wanted to make love to Anna but she wouldn't let me, though sometimes in the evening after the show, she would sit sipping Old Monk Gold Reserve mixed with Thums Up in her room, listening to Maria Callas, something that she remembered her father Boris indulging in at their Odessa home. "I do not understand it but I feel it, yes," she would say in her broken English and let me hold her hand. It was all very adolescent.'

'We usually stayed in a hotel called Kibbutz in Paharganj, it has a very famous Vedic terrace cafe called Madhuparka, which serves continental fare to all those who stop on the way to Pushkar, Manali and Rishikesh. In fact I have had a one-room flat there for the past three years. On some winter evenings, Anna liked to walk from Paharganj to Central Park and then around the Inner Circle. I usually accompanied her on these walks. We would invariably stop at Volga for a quick beer and a dinner of Chicken a la Kiev and Russian Salad. She had never eaten those when she was in Russia. Imagine. They must have been really poor. We would then walk back the same way, working off the heavy dinner. She wouldn't ever take an autorickshaw, she loved the walk she said. Cleared her head. Stopped her from thinking about her mum and younger sister with whom she had lost touch. Besides she felt safe walking with me. I was her "protector" she said. She is also very spiritual. Around Diwali we were in Bombay and we had a day off. I decided to visit Shirdi to pay my respects to Sai Baba, Anna insisted on coming along with me. I even tied the red string mouli with the Sai Baba locket on her right wrist.'

'Jishnu da, do you think we can order some Chicken a la Kiev?'

'No. It is the Pitri Paksha. I am off any kind of meat except pussy.'

'All right. Just checking.' I was so dejected that I didn't have the heart to inform Jishnu da that it was already December.

The trouble in the Footfalls Dance Company started about a month back when Svetlana suddenly decided that she had had enough of India and wanted to strike out on her own. She knew the business now and had decided she didn't need Jindal or the Footfall Dance Company anymore. She knew that she would be able to find dancers of her own. She wanted to move on to bigger things. She wanted to move back to London and from there run the North African tour. A one-eyed Berber camel dealer Svetlana had met at the Sun-n-Sand Hotel in Bombay had promised to set her up. North Africa was where the real money was and they really loved their blondes down in Marrakesh. Far more than in India.

The Berber had already leased a flat for her in Chelsea and he wanted her to come to London as soon as possible. So even though Svetlana and Anna had over five months of contract left to fulfill, Svetlana decided to leave. Naturally, when Jindal came to know he freaked out. He said no. Here was this girl whom he truly loved fucking and had also started depending upon emotionally, spent so much money on, and with whom he had seen dreams of a long glorious future, suddenly one morning she looks up from doing her Wonder Woman in mid-flight act and says, 'Darling! I leave India now. I go back to London, yes.' Jindal beats her up badly. Dislocated shoulder, cracked rib, couple of broken fingers. The works. She is in intensive care at a private nursing home in Pitampura for a week. Jindal won't let her go and there is one major problem. The passports of all the girls are deposited with Jindal for the duration of their contract. As soon as they land in India their passports are taken by Jindal and kept in a safe in his office in Shankar Market. Svetlana and Anna must have their European passports to leave the country. The one week that Svetlana spends in the nursing home, Anna is constantly by her side. Soon she goes to her protector asking for help. Jishnu da agrees but with one caveat, that she stay back and marry him. Anna does not agree. She does not see herself making litti-chokha in Kadam Kuan, Patna. She wants to leave with Svetlana. Jishnu da reiterates the offer. God has finally given him a chance to claim Anna for his own and he is not giving it up. He knows he is taking an enormous risk, plotting against Jindal, who has links with every police officer and politician of any standing in Delhi. But nothing is more important than Anna. The next day Anna agrees. She probably realizes that Jishnu da is her only hope of getting Svetlana out of Jindal's clutches ever. For her nothing is more important than Svetlana's safety. Jishnu da would get Svetlana's passport out from Jindal's safe and after she has flown the coop, Anna and Jishnu da would disappear together. 'Maybe we will go back to Patna.' They plan carefully. Jishnu da makes all the travel arrangements, books Svetlana's ticket. And she is supposed to fly in two hours' time from Indira Gandhi International Airport. While I was getting a shave earlier in the evening, Jishnu da had opened up Jindal's safe and taken out her passport. By early morning Jindal would know. Jishnu da is the only one besides him who knows the combination. No money is kept in the safe, only passports and documents and photos of the girls.

'Here's the passport,' Jishnu da kept the deep maroon passport on the table and I picked it up and looked at Svetlana Vorsin's photograph and looking at her could never have guessed her fascinating story. But then you never do from passport photos. She looked like any other firang girl, unwashed and dazed by the crowds, one sees walking along Janpath being trailed by chattering touts with crazy bright eyes.

'The troupe is performing at Marina Hotel around the corner at the moment. Ten minutes back Svetlana probably left for the airport. And in the next ten minutes I should get a call from Anna who will come and pick me up from outside Volga. So goodbye now, Hriday, dear old friend, I always liked you, even though you are such a loser. Wear a Pukhraj on your right forefinger. If you can afford one that is. Your Shani is weak. You have a good heart, though. One last drink now.' Jishnu da signalled to the waiter for two double whiskies.

By this time, with the heady combination of ganja, beer and Peter Scot I was so drunk that I felt as if I was living somebody else's life. This morning I would have never guessed my day would turn out like this. My eyes were out of focus. I was hearing everything through an echo and I was sure when I got up, my legs would give away and I would fall on the thick wine-coloured pile and drop off to a well-deserved sleep.

Just then Jishnu da's large Motorola mobile rang.

'Right on time. It is Anna outside. Goodbye now, Hriday.' Jishnu da got up and put a couple of thousand-rupee notes on the table, leaving a generous tip.

I too got up then and my legs incredibly did manage to take up my weight.

'Jishnu da, I want to look at Anna once, if it is all right?' Jishnu da looked at me and smiled and said, 'once a chutpal, always a chutpal', then motioned with his hand to follow him.

A kaali-peeli Ambassador taxi with an ancient Sardarji at the wheels was standing outside. The street was wet with rain. In the back seat of it sat Anna Kuchma, still the prettiest girl I have ever seen or will see. Jishnu da walked up to her and said, 'Anna there has been a change in the plans.' As she looked up with eyes full of despair at him, Jishnu da took out two passports instead of one and gave them to her along with the ticket.

'Here you go. You are both free now. Don't say anything. Just leave. There is little time before check-in ends.'

Anna started opening the door but Jishnu da firmly closed it back and tapped the taxi driver on the shoulder. There was a flash of lightning and I noticed the frayed red mouli from Shirdi on her right wrist.

As the taxi turned a corner and faded into the Delhi night I lit a Gold Flake and then after a few puffs passed it to Jishnu da like we used to do in our Shokeen Niwas days.

'When did you decide you would let Anna go?'

'When I was telling you her story. About half an hour back. Right when the hippie couple at the next table left. The girl had her arms around the boy's waist. I just realized that she loved Svetlana so much and it is a crime to separate lovers.

At the back of my mind I had known it all along.'

'What will you do about Jindal?'

'I will disappear in the next few minutes. Maybe Jindal will find me, maybe not. If he does, I will always have this, won't I?' And then Jishnu da pulled out a Mauser, perhaps the same one with which, centuries back, he had shot at Prachi Jindal's car and made her a star.

'Can I do anything for you?'

'Write about me.' And saying that Jishnu da turned and walked rapidly towards the outer galleries of neon-lit Connaught Place and soon disappeared into the slowly curling wisp of blue smoke from my Gold Flake, bringing the curtain down on the derelict day.

# The Changing of the Guard}

The year was 1997 and I was twenty-two years old. A year had passed since I had my M.A. in English from Hindu College in Delhi University. I had missed making the first division by 2 per cent but by English Literature standards it was not such a big disgrace. After my M.A. I had gone back to my hometown Patna to prepare for the civil services as I didn't want to do an M.Phil and pursue a career in academics. I felt I didn't have the patience nor the crazy-bright zeal that a teacher of literature should necessarily have for such an august profession. With civil services I could go back to Patna and save my family the fairly stiff monthly expense of staying in Delhi. Father had retired from his professorship in the English department, Darbhanga House a few months back. Though still well off, the family didn't have money like before. Also I needed a job quickly so that I could marry Charulata Roy but then anyone could have told me that the civil services were certainly not the correct option for a man in such a hurry. Surprisingly, no one did.

A year of preparing for the civils convinced me of my folly. That one year in Patna was spent writing stories and reading the entire modern literature section of the British Council Library. Even though for the first couple of months I did maintain the pretence of studying for the civils, I gave that up as I sank deeper and deeper into a phase of monumental indecision. But I did complete about three short stories, of which I was quite proud for some time. The stories were of Charulata and the time spent with her. It was more an act of remembering than fiction and when I read those unpublished stories today I realize how intensely I missed Charulata that year when we had voluntarily chosen to stay apart. She in Delhi pursuing her M.Phil in Modern Indian History and I in Patna writing stories and brooding about my deeply uncertain future.

The only certain thing in my life was Charulata. I had met her when I was in M.A (Previous). I was then at Hindu and she was in St Stephen's and we met through mutual friends from Patna. She was from Dhanbad, a small town in south Bihar, now in Jharkhand, known for its many defunct collieries and the raging fire smouldering in its bowels.

A bit about Charulata now. The first thing one noticed about her, apart from her large Durga-shaped eyes, was her nose which set the tone for her personality. So even though she was not more than 5 feet 4 inches tall in her thick-soled Chinese flip-flops, she was, I felt, forever looking down at me. A kulin Bengali of the Vaidya caste, fluent for some strange reason in Bhojpuri (her father, a general surgeon, had been posted in Ara for a long time in her childhood, I came to know later), she liked singing ribald Bhojpuri marriage songs and playing the dholak. And it was in that avatar I had first seen her on Holi in 1995. I, along with a couple of my friends, had gone to the Mall Apartments on Mall Road, where in one of the servants' quarter blocks stayed a group of girls from Bihar in adjacent rooms. One of the girls, Swastika Singh, was a cousin of my childhood friend Pranjal Sinha. The atmosphere, as you can believe, was raucous, as a group of ten or twelve boys and girls soaked in a rainbow of colours and poteen sat singing Holi songs.

*Rama khele Holi*
*Lachman khele Holi*
*Lanka dahan ho to*
*Ravan khele Holi*

Charulata was the witch with silver poteen-smeared hair who sang the songs as we all joined in the chorus. Thandai laced with Azadpur Mandi bhang and Blue Riband gin and Limca was going around along with the maal pua and fiery red mutton curry that the girls had cooked on their multipurpose electric heater. Charulata had recently shifted to the room adjacent to Swastika di's with another girl from Dhanbad. But it was only in the evening when Pranjal and I went to Swastika di's to put abeer on her feet and do the obligatory pranam that I noticed the eyes and that nose of the freshly scrubbed Charulata Roy and promptly fell in love. A week later I met her outside her lecture hall in Stephen's and over mince cutlets and nimbu pani at the cafe asked her out to a movie the following Saturday. The movie was the Guru Dutt-Waheeda Rehman classic *Pyaasa*. We took the Teevra Mudrika from the Mall Road bus stop outside her room and reached Pragati Maidan half an hour before the twelve o'clock show. As we bought the twelve-rupee tickets and waited for the gates to open, she fed me and herself golgappas from a thela nearby. She must have consumed at least twenty. Which was a good thing as what with my borrowed budget of 150 rupees for the date, I had barely enough for lunch and the auto ride back home to the university in the evening. She had made it very clear that she wouldn't take a crowded bus in the evening. So that's how it went and later that year when a vacancy came up in Charulata's block I moved into a servant's quarters on the first floor. She lived on the third.

A year went by wherein our love grew and we decided to get married in the near future. I still remember the day I proposed to her. It was December and I was in Patna for the winter vacations and Charu was in Dhanbad. In the morning while having breakfast, my father suffered a mild heart attack and I drove him to the Kurji Holy Family Hospital where he was kept in the ICU till evening. It was a terrible day and all through it I had been in shock and praying to god that he should save my father somehow. In the evening, when he was finally shifted to a private room from the ICU, I left my mother alone with him and went out to the small bazaar near the hospital gate and called Charulata at home.

I told her about my father and then in the same breath asked her if she would marry me. She was taken aback, to say the very least. I was whispering, she told me later, she couldn't hear me properly. I have no recollection of whispering. But she is probably correct. I was so emotionally overwrought at the time that I needed something permanent and I wanted to keep holding on to the one thing that I treasured most in my life apart from my parents. It took a crisis like my father's illness to see with clarity what I wanted most in life and that was Charulata Roy. Fortunately she said yes. I quickly put the phone down lest she change her mind.

So in the summer of 1997 when I had already spent about nine months apart from Charulata, I informed her that when she was in Dhanbad for her vacations, I would come over and meet her parents. Make my intentions clear so to say. A week earlier she had written to me that a marriage proposal from a family friend had come for her. When she was next in Dhanbad, she would have to meet the boy. It would be discourteous not to. But she would say no to him, she promised. He was a trainee civil engineer at Tata Steel. Charulata was not so enthused about my coming over to Dhanbad. She felt it was all a bit premature and I had a feeling that she was plain nervous. But nine months in isolation—when our only modes of communication were a couple of letters a week and a phone call every weekend—had made it very clear to me that coming back to Patna and the forced separation had been a bad decision all round. Also her apparent lack of enthusiasm made me question her commitment. Perhaps she was having second thoughts about a man who wanted to be a writer and probably would be poor all his life. I refused to countenance the fact that she was only twenty-one years old and had her feet more firmly placed on the ground than me. She reminded me of Supriya Chowdhury in *Meghe Dhaka Tara*. Mostly the stoicism, not the sadness. I never told her that.

Brushing all her protestations aside I went to the railway station and booked a sleeper berth on Saturday evening's Ganga-Damodar with the return on Sunday evening. I would reach Dhanbad early in the morning, spend the day with Charu and return the same day. When I told my parents about my decision to marry Charulata, they didn't raise any objections even though she was of a different caste and they had never met her. But even they were not very comfortable about my going to Dhanbad and meeting her parents on my own. They would have preferred it if her parents had made the first overture and visited Patna. But I knew I didn't have time for such protocol as I had to claim Charu for myself at the earliest. To their credit they didn't even point to the glaring fact of my acute joblessness. They probably realized looking at me that I was beyond all manner of embarrassment at that point in time. The months of separation and now this proposal from a 'family friend' had made me somewhat paranoid.

I had got an RAC ticket which got confirmed after I boarded the train. I had got an aisle lower berth and I opened both the windows and read Turgenev's *A Sportsman's Sketches*. A book which always calms me down and makes me feel more generously disposed towards humanity in general. In the night the breeze from both the windows cooled the compartment and it was good to read about Turgenev's aristocratic Russia by the light of the Eveready pocket torch.

I couldn't sleep. After midnight I closed the book, smoked Gold Flakes and brooded about Charulata and my life. Whether it was such a good idea to get married so early and also whether I would get a suitable job. I thought about my improbable dream of becoming a published writer some day and I knew everything, all my happiness, depended upon two crucial things, that I should marry Charulata and then hopefully write a book of stories that was publishable. To me it was all connected.

To keep writing I needed Charulata and to keep Charulata I had to keep writing because my being a writer was a huge part of her attraction for me. There are some generous girls in this world who will only love writers and Charu was one of them. She was the eternal writer's wife. So the first thing was to marry her and the rest would necessarily follow. With the help of such logic, my fragile resolve recharged once more, I dozed off finally in the early morning. When I woke up, the train had reached Dhanbad station and half of the compartment had already disembarked. I got down and saw

Charulata further up on the platform standing shyly by a magazine stall, wearing the cream and red Cottage Emporium sari I had bought her from Janpath. This was a surprise. Putting the Turgenev into my shoulder bag, I walked towards her. I had not expected her to receive me at the station. I had told her that I would take a rickshaw and reach her Luby Circular Road home on my own. But it was good to see her after such a long time. She told me that her father had driven her to the station and was now waiting in the parking area. Dr Roy, dressed in white shorts and a T-shirt, was cleaning the windshield of his car with a multi-coloured feather duster. He greeted me with an awkward handshake as I made to touch his feet, and then asked me to sit in front with him. Dr Roy was on his way to his morning game of badminton at the Dhanbad Club. Once in a while, driving the white-coloured Premier Padmini, he would point out the local sights: 'Ah, the Circuit House on your left.' He asked me about Patna and the worsening law and order situation there. Things were still much better in south Bihar. But it was only a matter of time he felt that a new state would be carved out for south Bihar and they would be rid of Laloo Prasad Yadav. After dropping us off at the front gates of his house Dr Roy went off to the Dhanbad Club nearby.

Charu's mother was distinctly uncomfortable while meeting me but solicitously asked me about the journey and then instructed Charu to show me the bathroom so that I could freshen up. Up until now I hadn't had a solitary moment with Charu and as we went up the stairs to the first floor I asked Charu about her prospective suitor.

'Don't worry about him. He is nothing to me. I would have rejected him anyway. Like I told you. There was no need to panic, Hriday. But I guess just as well. There is a bit of friction with Mum regarding your visit but I am sure everything will be all right.' Her tone though was uncertain and then she hugged me and gave me a quick kiss on the lips.

After my bath, I went down for breakfast, buoyed by Charu's wholesome kiss and reassurance. By then I was already feeling like a newly minted jamai babu and quite proprietorial. I ate ten puris in a flash and only stopped when Charulata arched her eyebrows. She could do that well. The visit in general went off well I thought. After breakfast Charu's mother asked me subtle questions about my education and ambition in life and when I told her that I wanted to become a novelist, she said that she was very pleased for me, that, here she looked meaningfully at Charu, 'for Charu's sake I hope you succeed.' Charu laughed and said in a teasing manner, 'Ma, even if he did I do not think he would ever earn enough to keep me in the style I deserve to be kept.' The uncertainty in her voice was gone now. I felt that the sheer audacity of my act of turning up at their doorstep had won Mrs Roy over to my side. We spent the forenoon drinking lemonade and listening to old Talat Mahmood albums on the Philips record player.

*Itna na mujhse tu pyaar badha*
*Ki main ek badal awaara.*

And

*Sham-e-gham ki kasam*
*Aaj ghamgeen hain ham.*

Mahmood's mellifluous melancholia couldn't put a dampener on my ever-soaring mood. Dr Roy had joined us by now.

He told me about Charu's suitor, the trainee engineer from Jamshedpur, who unknown to himself was now eliminated in the first round because of me.

I assured Dr Roy that I would get a job soon, probably in journalism or publishing and that he wouldn't have to worry about Charu anymore. I proclaimed profoundly that 'my only ambition in life is to marry Charulata Roy', a statement that drew incredulous and loud laughter from the entire Roy family.

'You have a year, to get a suitable job. Then we will see,' Dr. Roy said to me in the evening while I was leaving for the station. He then passed the keys of the car to Charulata.

Charu drove me to the station in the Premier Padmini. This time round Dr Roy didn't accompany us. I felt as if the changing of the guard had already taken place. The marriage was now only a formality and all was right with the world. My optimism was such.

# Autobiography}

Siddharth Chowdhury is thirty-one years old and has published a novel that no one has actually read. Not to mention an earlier collection of short stories which sank like the proverbial stone. It had his photo on the cover and is now a collector's item. No wonder. He is bearded and bald and built like an over the hill middle-weight. Even though he lives somewhere in South Delhi, his friends do not yet call him 'Sid'.

But since he fancies himself as a novelist, he does on some frosty winter evenings, after a couple of pegs of super strong Hercules XXX Rum, bought from a shady theka near Ashram Chowk, wish for the kind of success that *would* necessarily go straight to his head. A success after which hopefully everyone would start whispering 'Sid Rocks'. And how. Chowdhury sometimes suffers from delusions of grandeur.

Every morning, sharp at six, Siddharth wakes up and plays Kishori Amonkar on his computer. Usually Raga Basant Bahar. She is more effective than Bloody Mary he feels. At 6.30 he is ready for the day. He usually wears a battered old herringbone jacket that will soon need to be patched with leather from his Zakir Husain College days, over a bottle-green Nike sweatshirt and faded Wrangler jeans. His feet are shod in slightly scuffed brown brogues. It is a quality shoe. Chowdhury thinks of himself as a sharp dresser.

After tying a tartan muffler, he sits at the dining table trying to work on a ten-line poem he has been writing for the past two weeks. Till now he has got two lines done. A line a week. He thinks it to be a good progress. He writes with yellow Staedtler pencils (134 HB) on natural shade prescription pads. A month or two more and he would have the poem licked.

7.20, he puts the pencil in his jacket pocket and goes into the kitchen. At 7.30, he has a single hard-boiled egg with two slices of toasted white bread. Thick Amul butter spread evenly on both slices. He brews a small pot of very sweet, heavy on milk, tea to wash it down. On a brass Leningrad samovar that once belonged to his mother. On its sides, below the spout, it depicts a pastoral engraving of Russian women in scarves stacking sheaves of barley.

7.45, he walks briskly out of his housing colony. He finds the early morning chill and wraparound Delhi fog invigorating.

Two of his neighbours, Chaddha and Chawla, are up and doing their bit for the South Delhi parking wars. Sullen school children with sleepy-eyed mothers wait for their buses near the back gate. Siddharth takes a shortcut through the nearby gurudwara to reach the Ring Road bus stop, from where he will catch the Teevra Mudrika to Rajghat. The gurudwara is quite special to him, its air of eternal calm and early morning piety always lifts his spirits up.

He works in a publishing house. His office is on Ansari Road, where all the publishers are. Oxford, Macmillan, Rupa, Manohar, Picador, Cambridge, Tangent, Proscenium, among many, many others. From Rajghat it is a five-minute walk. His is the room at the top.

7.55, Chowdhury buys a pack of Gold Flake Kings from Tripurari Pandey, who hands him a clutch of Hajmola candies in lieu of the requisite change. Tripurari is from Sonepur, across the Ganga from Patna, Siddharth's hometown, and plies his trade by the side of the bus stop.

After waving off three partly filled up Mudrikas, Siddharth gets on one which is almost empty and has all its windows intact.

8.05, Sarai Kale Khan Bus Terminal. A beggar girl gets on the bus and starts crawling on all fours towards him. She has cataract in one of her out-of-focus pale green eyes. She is probably on smack. Before she can press his feet in a knowing way, Siddharth drops the Hajmola candies into her extended hand. Astonished she catches all of it thinking it to be loose change. One of these days Siddharth will ask her her name. Chowdhury is a collector of names.

As the bus leaves Sarai Kale Khan, a spare man in a shiny wine-coloured three-piece suit, which he probably got stitched for his wedding, jumps on, and in a voice perfect for selling biscuits, says 'Attention!' as if he were at a parade ground.

Farid Khan is not a vendor of biscuits. He is a vendor of books. Like Siddharth. They are from the same trade. Farid is from Agra. One of his ancestors engraved a panel of aayat on the Taj Mahal. It took him three and a half years. Siddharth thinks it to be a good progress. Today Farid is selling a *Delhi Tourist Guide*. For five rupees. After Siddharth buys one, four more get sold.

8.25, Rajghat. Gandhi Baba's resting place. Chowdhury takes *HT City* out of his green canvas bag and spreads it on his favourite iron bench to soak up the dew. If he can't be on Page 3, at least he can sit on it. You are no one in Delhi if you are not on Page 3. Surely. All round him joggers move about in quiet desperation. He admires a magnificent bullmastiff with an ungainly owner. He worries for a bit about the dog's soul.

It always cheers up Siddharth immensely whenever he watches the human race battle against the ravages of time. He himself has lost the battle a long time back. The mastiff comes and curls up at his feet. Tongue hanging out. The sun too has come out. Siddharth lifts his face to the sunshine. For several seconds his eyes close. He rummages inside his magical bag for the book of the day. It is the Cyril Connolly classic *Enemies of Promise*. The 1979 Penguin Modern Classic edition with a detail of Eton College Chapel on the cover.

A good choice and Chowdhury would do well to read it carefully.

9.00 a.m. He is in his room at the top and all is well with the world.

# Damsel in Distress}

Truth be told I am attracted to big-breasted women and the girl sitting diagonally opposite me at Pindi Sweet House in Kilokri near Maharani Bagh had tits that would delight even the great Jogen Chowdhury. Not for me the size zero look that is all the rage these days. I like women who look like women and not boys in drag. The girl, who was wearing a red Sarojini Nagar Adidas windcheater over a blue polo T-shirt and boot-cut stonewashed jeans, did not look more than eighteen and had a small black rucksack with Diesel emblazoned on the front kept at her feet. Pindi Sweet House was not a cafe where young unattended girls at 8.30 in the morning sat alone sipping a lukewarm cup of tea for fifteen minutes, while the two waiters kept staring and hovering around her yellow sunmica-topped table like hornets. The girl avoiding eye-contact with anyone kept looking at her thin gold-plated watch which was shaped like a bangle, and held on to her fast dwindling cup of tea realizing that the moment she would put the cup back on the saucer, it would be whisked away. She is waiting for an errant boyfriend, I decided, and even though I was getting a faint vibration of distress from her, promptly lost interest in her. Apart from the two of us, there were no other customers at that hour.

Pindi Sweet House is an old-style mithai shop, where at the front is the steel and glass-encased sweets counter, with rows of gulab jamun, rasmalai, kaju katli and laddus in aluminum containers, and at the back are six to eight tables with straight-backed plastic chairs where patrons through the day usually have bread pakoras, samosas, chhole-bhature, with piping hot cups of tea. Here young lower-middle class couples with names like Pinky and Rocky bond over a shared plate of gulab jamuns in the evenings. I come to the cafe at least once a day. Usually for breakfast before catching the Teevra Mudrika from the Maharani Bagh bus stop for Arts Faculty in DU where I am pursuing an M.Phil on the revenue system of Balban. I cleared my JRF-NET in the first attempt and now on the princely stipend paid by the government of India I manage quite well. I must admit that I am terribly bright. I stay in a barsati nearby and from my terrace you can have a grand view of the Ring Road, Ashram Chowk, the NAFED building and Mathura Road. At nights after consuming a quarter bottle of Old Monk, I sit and stare at the long line of inter-state buses and goods-laden lorries from every part of India that for a moment by their presence make my meagre universe larger. I feel like Kaikobad then, standing at the ramparts of his now vanished fort at Kilokri, staring intensely at the Yamuna, where he liked to disport with his concubines. Did he ever have a premonition that one day soon he would be wrapped up in a carpet with intricate Persian motifs of paradise and thrown into his beloved Yamuna, to be lost in its still water depths? Perhaps not, but looking at the neon-lit frenzy of the Ring Road I am sure to die by its side one day. I think of death a lot and I hate to travel. There are days when even this five-minute walk to the Pindi Sweet House from my room is an ordeal. I like to sit and stare.

I came to Delhi about six months back in May after my

Masters from Vinoba Bhave University, Hazaribagh. Delhi is still a new place for me. I am still getting used to its rhythms but the mofussil slowness still clings to me like a burr. I wish I could shed it fast, this slowness, which when I observe my merry classmates, I feel is holding me back socially. For one it makes me excruciatingly shy, when it comes to women. I like women and instantly connect with them. I can hear their inner thoughts but try as I might I can't seem to open myself up to them. When I see the women in my group, many of whom are in relationships, some longstanding, others ephemeral, I too want to enter their world, so full of lightness. I am bored with wearing my heart on my sleeve for so long, I want to wear a condom now, for a change. The attraction I have felt for some of my female colleagues has at times made me extremely restless. If better sense had not prevailed, last Tuesday morning I might have kissed Surma Kaneez, an exchange student from Sylhet, as she in her shallow-cut cotton T-shirt and sleeveless sweatshirt with the zipper undone bent down at the water faucet on the ground floor of the Arts Faculty to quench her desert thirst. It was like a flash, this intense desire to taste her lips. I could see her flesh-coloured bra strap from the side of her bare armpit. There is a fortnight's growth of fuzz there, which I could lovingly shave off with my Swiss Army knife, if she would only ask me. Even though her breasts are much smaller than what I usually like, I would have loved to open her bra at midnight in my barsati with my two nimble fingers and thus with her exposed at my side look down at the frenetic pace of traffic on the Ring Road like young gods. This desire was so extreme that as I watched droplets of water leak by the side of her wide wet mouth, on to her neck, I even forgot that she was a Muslim and I usually kept clear of them.

Before I left Hazaribagh my mother one day, in our Canary Hill Road cottage, told me while my father dozed on his rocking chair after an afternoon gin and lime that she would forgive everything but never a Muslim daughter-in-law. I am afraid my mother does behave like a bigot sometimes. It partly could be because her immediate family had to leave Sylhet a couple of years after partition. The family members who had chosen to stay back in East Pakistan had all converted to Islam over the years. There is no one I love more than my mother in this world. She also told me that I should be careful when it came to women as I am dangerously attractive to them. I am inclined to believe her. My mother has never lied to me. Truth be told I do have the kind of clean-cut regular face that women instinctively trust. I am also very fair. Just then Surma turned her head and looked at me. A hint of a bemused smile playing at the edge of those illicitly Saracenic lips. It is a smile I have come to know very well, following her photo updates regularly on Facebook. The same smile was there in a recent photograph she had uploaded of a party at her Hudson Lines flat, wherein Samar Sinha, one of our tutors, hugged her from behind. Even though she is bit of a dheeli chaddi, I could save her from the likes of Samar Sinha, if she would only let me. But then she never invites me to the parties she regularly throws. Aware of her incendiary gaze I quickly turned my back on the witch and ran up the staircase.

There are days when the loneliness gets so intense and claustrophobic that even my large terrace and Dostoevsky can't seem to alleviate it. I have to escape my barsati with its maroon-coloured sofa-cum-bed, coir mattress by the side and mango-wood writing table and chair, all lovingly bought by my mother from Amar Colony when she came to help me get settled in this strange land. There is a framed poster print of Jogen Chowdhury's *Sundari* on the wall, which I bought from the Lalit Kala Akademi stall at the Delhi Book Fair. The Sundari has breasts that look as if they can suckle the whole of humanity and still not tap out. Gazing at those raised grape-like nipples makes me feel warm and protected. Though when mum comes visiting I have to take down the painting and replace it with one of Vivekananda. I am afraid mother is not a very artistic type but then by her presence she makes me feel warm and protected and I do not have any need of *Sundari*. Beneath the poster is a small Godrej fridge alongside a 19-inch Samsung colour TV on a low floor book-case which has my text books and all of Dostoevsky. In my escape I usually walk to Defence Colony via Jangpura and Lajpat Nagar and then back after an anda paratha by the side of Eros Cinema Hall. Sometimes this frantic walk takes me two hours and if I am lucky about three. The best part is that after this exhausting walk my mind is free of all vexing thoughts about death and condoms that plague me through the day and I can fall asleep for a few hours. On good days I manage about four hours of sleep. Mostly it is three. On other nights I venture forth in the opposite direction. Towards Sarai Kale Khan bus terminal and the Indraprastha Park. In the night I love to run on the grounds of the deserted park in my new black-and-gold Adidas tracksuit. It reminds me of the Golden Jubilee Park near the central jail in Hazaribagh. I am a very fit person. There is not even an ounce of fat anywhere on my body and there is a ten-inch difference between my waist and shoulders. 'While my son has a six-pack, I have a family-pack,' my father frequently says in a jocular fashion to his friends after a couple of drinks, as always my perfection a grim reminder of his own full-blown mediocrity.

The only problem with Indraprastha Park is that at night you meet all sorts of degenerate and desperate characters. The police I believe should be more vigilant. This is a family park. A few nights back just as I was about to enter the park, a comely hijra suddenly appeared out of the shrubs and said to me 'thoda sucking? thoda fucking?' and I promptly without bothering to reply to the filthy suggestions took out my Swiss Army knife, a present from my mother on my fifteenth birthday nine years back, and held it at the hijra's neck. She caught hold of my hand and believe me these creatures are pretty strong. But I pulled her hair back and was about to make a smallish cut on her Nycil powdered neck, then somehow I came to my senses and loosened my grip on her. In a flash she wrenched herself free and disappeared into the night. Stirred not shaken, I continued on to my run. A couple of days before that, midway into my run I heard some voices from the covered pavilion that is right in the middle of the park. I thought I heard a faint female shriek for help. Sometimes even at nights when I am sleeping, I hear this piercing shriek, a woman calling out to me from somewhere, for help. I wake up then. Cold sweat all over my body.

In the pavilion I found a young couple on the floor, the girl still in her school uniform, with her nylon zebra striped chaddi and salwar around her knees and the boy bare assed on top of her. Without thinking of consequences I ran in to save the girl and gave the boy a tremendous kick on his back-side which sent him sprawling across the floor. The girl started saying 'please, please, please' and the boy, snub-nosed and pimply, pulling up his skinny jeans tried to run away. But not before some choice slaps from yours truly in the still of the night, which went off like gunfire. The boy though muscular didn't fight back. The shock and awe was too much for him. I had descended like the wrath of God on them. The girl meanwhile had started dialling a number on her mobile and I left the boy and moved quickly over to the girl and snatched her mobile phone. 'This is a family park. My children play here,' I screamed at her. The boy ran away quickly, leaving the girl behind. 'Don't ever come back here,' I warned the girl and she with tear-filled eyes nodded in affirmation. I ordered her to pull at her own ears and do uthak-baithak. After she had done about five, I let her go. I switched off her mobile phone. Yesterday, feeling restless while reading *Notes from the Underground*, I saw the mobile phone on the lower shelf of the bookcase. I picked it up and switched it on. She hadn't yet blocked her SIM card. I wonder why. The girl's name was Ritu Bisht and there was a Pandav Nagar address given below. This was the first thing that came on the display when the phone was switched on. I went to her messages and most of them were from a certain Goldy. And they were filthy, filthy, filthy. I switched the phone off and put it in my laptop bag for future reference.

'Are you done? Shall I take this away?' The waiter leaned and asked the girl in the Adidas jacket pointedly. His right hand already touching the saucer. The girl put the cup back on the saucer and said softly, 'Of course.'

'Shall I bring another cup of tea? Or a plate of bread pakoras perhaps?' The waiter Dubey who was from Sultanpur persisted, taking obvious pleasure in the girl's embarrassment. The owner whom I called Chaddha-Chawla looked benevolently from the counter.

'No, I am waiting for someone. Perhaps later.'

'Madam, if you are waiting, you will have to order something. Rules,' Dubey nodded towards Chaddha-Chawla and said to the girl.

This was getting to be too much. I had to step in and save the girl I felt.

'Pandit, bring my sister another cup of tea. One by two,' I raised my own cup and said to the waiter in my strong foghorn of a voice. As Dubey walked away crestfallen, I smiled reassuringly at the girl. I might not have mentioned it earlier but I do have a smile that women instinctively trust. The girl, somewhat flustered, started to protest but then, looking at my face and feeling my special power, thought otherwise.

As Dubey, eyes twinkling like a marionette, placed the cup of tea in front of her, the girl quickly looked at me and said 'thank you'. I carried my cup of tea over to her table and before she could protest, sat down facing her. Dubey looked at me aghast as Chaddha-Chawla broadly smiled and winked at me. Oh how I can't for the life of me abide these lower-middle class bastards.

'I couldn't help noticing that you were frightened of something. Is someone following you? You can tell me. I will take care of it,' I said to the girl in my quiet and sincere manner.

'No, no, it is nothing like that. You are mistaken. I am just waiting for a friend. He should be here anytime now.'

'Are you sure? You can trust me.'

'It is the truth. I am just a bit tired. I had fever for the past two days. I am on antibiotics.'

'And still you came to meet him. He must be very special.'

'Yes, we are getting married today.'

Ah! So she had run away from her home. And gradually

over slow sips of the over-sweet adrak ki chai, I ferreted out her story which looking at her stonewashed jeans I had known couldn't be anything but mundane. Her name was Satnam and she had passed her twelfth standard exams a few months before. She stayed in Lajpat Nagar with her parents and two elder brothers and they had a grocery store in one of the by-lanes of Central Market. She had met Rocky a year back in Surajkund when she had gone there on a school trip.

'He has a very good outlook,' she blushed and explained to me. What she meant was that he was very good looking. With that kind of name, he probably shaves his chest hair and wears a baseball cap all the time I instantly thought. It is the kind of pseudo-Western Christian sounding name I regularly use in self-service restaurants like Nirula's and Wimpy. 'Mr. Johnny, your footlong is ready.' Johnny, Johnny? Yes, Papa? Eating Sugar? No, Papa. To have those glorified waiters behind the counter utter my kulin Brahmin name would be an absolute outrage. Rocky and Satnam had exchanged numbers and later after many forwarded messages and conversations late into the night, she had one evening met him at the Indraprastha Park and their love had blossomed. But last week while coming out of the Centre Stage Mall in Noida with Rocky, she was spotted by her elder brother Lovely and his friends. They thrashed Rocky very badly and took her forcibly home. She had been locked in her home for the past one week. Her mobile was confiscated. But yesterday evening she got a message from her best friend that Rocky would meet her at 8 a.m. at Pindi Sweet House. So at night she put Calmpose in her mother's glass of milk and early in the morning she slipped out of the house with thirty rupees in her pocket and a rucksack which had a few pieces of jewellery and her school-leaving certificate. She had waited at the Maharani Bagh bus stand and when the Pindi Sweet House finally opened at 7.30 was the first one in along with the staff.

Looking at her closely, I realized that she was a very attractive girl. Sharp-featured, fair with light-coloured eyes that Punjabis from Lahore and beyond sometimes have, she had, up close I could see, magnificent breasts. I was not wrong. Sipping my tea I mused how she would look standing bare-breasted beside me on the terrace at night. I could cover her with my Jaipuri razai with its intricate patterns of paradise, if it got too chilly. Then I thought that the girl was a damsel in distress and I shouldn't be having such thoughts about her. I was sent to save her and not fuck her. I should focus on helping her. Even though I was very careful, the girl probably noticed that I was staring at her breasts, so she self-consciously zipped up her jacket. Mum says women have an in-built radar for such things.

'Rocky should be here soon. Thank you so much for helping me.'

'Are you sure he is coming for you? Maybe he has got cold feet. What does he do?' I said to her in my natural Brahminical doublespeak. Ambiguity and native cunning, necessary ingredients from my kulin heritage.

'He will come. He loves me. He is not the sort to get cold feet. He has a mobile phone repair shop near Jeevan Hospital. He also sells recharge. Vodafone, Airtel, Idea, MTNL. Also Tata Sky.' The girl seemed more nervous now than she had five minutes back.

'You know, I think you should go home, Satnam,' I said to the girl in my sincere manner.

'No, please don't say that. I can't go home now. He will

come for me.' Satnam started crying and I felt tremendously guilty at having caused her more distress. Mum would so disapprove.

Chaddha-Chawla was, I could see, listening in very carefully now.

'Why don't you give him a call? Maybe he is still sleeping?' I again flashed my ever so reassuring smile.

'You know they have taken away my mobile,' the girl said to me sharply and more tears flowed from her green-coloured eyes.

'Here, use mine.' I put my hand in my jacket pocket and was about to take out my mobile phone when I suddenly remembered the phone I had confiscated from the dheeli chaddi in Indraprastha Park. It was in my laptop bag. I unzipped the bag and took out the mobile. I switched it on and gave it to the girl.

Satnam dialled the number of her boyfriend and it rang for a long time but Rocky didn't pick up.

'Call him again in five minutes. He is probably taking a bath.' It had been a very long time since I had spoken to a girl at such length and I was enjoying it. So this is how it will be when I get married. I was not feeling shy anymore. Mum was right. It would go away one day, she had promised.

'Who is Ritu Bisht?'

'Ritu Bisht?'

'The name on the display?'

'Oh, right, yes, of course. Ritu is my girlfriend. She forgot her phone in my room last evening. I will return it to her when she comes to meet me in half an hour. In fact I should be going soon. Don't want to keep her waiting.'

'Have you two been together long?'

'It will be a year on Christmas day. We are planning to get married next year. There is opposition from her parents. She is from Garhwal, I am from Assam. You know? But they will come through in the end. Our love is very strong. On my side there is no problem, my mother is very broad-minded. My father died in my childhood.'

'You are from Assam? You don't look like a Nepali.'

'No, my forefathers emigrated from the Doaba region in Punjab a long time back.'

Satnam nodded in an absent-minded manner and picked up the phone again. But the phone rang for a long time, nobody picked it up. The girl looked absolutely distraught now.

'Send him an SMS. He is probably not picking up the phone because he does not recognize the number. Tell him that you are waiting in Pindi Sweet House,' I suggested to the girl. 'Maybe he will call back.'

Satnam nodded and quickly sent an SMS to her boyfriend.

'I will have to leave soon. Why don't you come with me to my room and wait there. Ritu should be there soon and will be delighted to meet you. The view from the terrace is breathtaking.' And then I made the mistake of checking out her breasts again and the girl lowered her eyes and concentrated hard on the phone, willing it to ring. And then it did. The girl picked up the phone and said 'Rocky' and kept quiet as I could hear a male voice talking rapidly from the other side. A few seconds later the girl put the phone down and started crying again.

'What happened? He is not coming, is he?'

'My brothers are in Jeevan Nagar, looking for Rocky. He is hiding at a friend's place and as soon as he can slip away, he is coming to pick me up. He asked me to wait here and not to go out at any cost.'

'Well, I still think you should come with me to my room. The view…'

'No, please, no. I have to wait here. You can go now if you want. Thank you so much for all your help.' Satnam wouldn't even look at me now.

'No, of course not. I will wait with you and see no harm comes to you. It is my duty. You are my sister.' After that both of us kept quiet and waited at the cafe for Rocky. I called for another one by two tea. 'Rules.'

We didn't have to wait for long. Within fifteen minutes, a red Pulsar stopped right outside and a vaguely familiar young man of medium height with an orange baseball cap and a green and yellow Sarojini Nagar Ed Hardy sweatshirt came sprinting up the steps of the cafe. Satnam got up and picked up her rucksack. I got up too and extended my hand towards Rocky, who surprised, shook it vigorously.

'Bhaiyaji gave his phone to call you. He has been very helpful,' Satnam said to Rocky by way of introduction. Rocky, overcome by emotion, hugged me quickly. 'What is your name, brother? I already have your number. You must come home, bless your sister when everything is settled.'

'Goldy. My name is Goldy.'

'Thank you, Mr Goldy. Thank you.'

As both of them sat on the Pulsar and went on their way, Chaddha-Chawla came to the doorway and after a while said to me, 'You are a gentleman', and then he too shook my hand. Oh the soft cloying sentimentality of the lower-middle class.

'Did you recognize who the boy was?' he asked me.

'No.'

'He is Karim, of the Karim Meat Shop. Runs a mobile ki dukaan. He is local.'

'Right.'

Karim? Oh dear, I thought as I went back into the cafe. Mother would so disapprove.

# The Patna Manual of Style}

'Hriday Thakur is pretty no more', was the first thing that came to my mind as he received me, hand extended, in the Zakir Husain College staff room. But even with his receding hairline, those extra five kilos on that spare middle-weight frame, and that handlebar moustache from the Bihar badlands, I realized with a start that I still found him attractive and I always will. He is dressed as always, impeccably. Like a superannuated head boy. Dark-blue blazer, sky-blue shirt with cutaway collars and steel-grey trousers. Tie, burgundy with a single knot, and on his feet his favourite black brogues, buffed to perfection. Vain, vain man. Called to explain his pathological fastidiousness he would invariably say in his defiantly upper-class manner: 'It is the Patna courtly style, dear girl. You wouldn't understand.' And then, 'Go to any party, in any country, on any moonlit terrace of the world, the best dressed man is always the one from Patna.' Now go figure. It is good to know some things haven't changed.

I will be damned if I let him rectify a millenia's worth of separation with a mere handshake. We deserve better. I ignore the extended hand and give him a slow hug and kiss him on both cheeks. First left and then right. At first, startled, he laughs his merry head boy laugh and says softly, 'Anjali Singh Nalwa', like an incantation, and hugs me back. I love the spectacle, the drama of it and the fact that the proscenium arch today is the Zakir Husain staff room, the sanctum sanctorum of my growing up years. Also, I do it because Hriday, I think, when we were going out felt I was too undemonstrative of my love. But now I can do it, I can show him that I care and we have both come a long way. We are not the clueless adolescents we once were. A lot has happened since that year in Zakir. I have become a full-time novelist and mother and Hriday is an 'ad-hoc' lecturer in the English department at Zakir, with his book of stories forthcoming from Tangent. It was last Friday afternoon that I got the call from Hriday. 'I got your number from the Penguin office,' he explained. He wanted me to come and read my story 'Omkar' that had just been published in the new issue of *Biblio* to the Zakir Husain College Literary Society. This was Hriday's way of showing solidarity with me, I knew, as that morning it was in all the papers that the Government of India was contemplating bringing sedition charges against me for espousing pro-Khalistan sentiments in the story. Already a few copies of my novel *Adrift, Aloft* had been burned in Chitrakoot. I only hoped that they had paid for those copies. I had forgotten how calm and quiet his voice was and it was wonderful to know that dark December morning, that I still had old friends who cared for me. I accepted even though my feelings about my time spent in Zakir Husain remain ambivalent. They were in many ways miserable years and I was an emotional and social wreck those days. Writing was my passion and I was a girl in a hurry to get recognition and fame. I had no gift for friendship then. But now after a fairly well-received novel and another on the way I can finally call myself a writer in public without shame. The frenzy has abated somewhat and I can see with clear eyes how crucial my years in Zakir were. It is here that I finally began to write like a writer.

For an incredible 1,200 rupees a year, I got an education that transformed a deeply troubled eighteen-year-old lower-middle class girl with stars in her eyes into a serious novelist who never looked back after her years here. In the staff room I found around myself all the teachers who had made me a novelist. The gracious and ever compassionate Lima Kanungo who taught me that 'a novelist is many things but never a PRO'. Anuradha Marwah, fine novelist herself and still stunning after all these years, who said to me one day while marking a story I had written that 'a writer is never, never middle class'. Uday Chowdhury, the Joyce scholar on whom I had such a crush, told me after reading a story on the Sikh carnage of 1984 that 'a writer is always a dissident. He can't help but be on the left. He is too uncertain to be on the right.' As I stood in that staff room clutching Hriday's hand and looking at all my teachers, I felt a surge of gratitude. Something which my temperament does not allow too often.

It was right here that I had got the education to be what I always wanted to be. I was glad that they had asked me to come back and read 'Omkar'.

I read the story to a packed classroom full of students from all three years. It was in the same large first floor classroom that Hriday and I had met for the first time when I asked him to sing the national anthem during ragging.

Before I read 'Omkar', a few students read portions from *Adrift, Aloft* that were set in the college. Their awkward yet endearing rendition made me feel very grateful and the sense of despondency I had felt ever since last Friday lifted off me as if by magic. I read calmly but was acutely aware of Hriday's presence, just a few inches away from me. Only thinking of the virtue of the students had I let go of his hand while reading. All the while reading 'Omkar' I hoped that he noticed that my hair was long again, the way it was when we first met and used to take those long bus rides on Route 901.

After the reading Hriday and I mingled with the students and faculty over coffee and samosas.

'Are you afraid of going to jail, Ms Nalwa?' Hriday asked me, half in jest I thought.

'I am terrified,' I told him truthfully.

'Then why do you write such stories?'

'Because that is what I do. I am a writer and not a copywriter.'

'You will be all right. You should realize that you must be really good if the government of the day is afraid of you. If you must know I am terribly envious of you.'

'I just want to be read. Same as you.'

After it all got over, Hriday walked me to the college gate and passed me an envelope with five hundred rupees in it. 'Conveyance, for taxi. We pay all our guests. You remember,' Hriday explained.

'I am not taking a taxi. I am taking the Route 901 bus.'

'But you do not stay in the university anymore.'

'No, but you do. Gwyer Hall. I googled.'

Hriday laughed his merry head boy laugh and hand in hand we crossed over to the other side and waited for our very own 901.

# Goat-Getting}

There was a time not long back when any man with *Eleven Kinds of Loneliness* on his shelves would invariably get my goat. Then Leonardo came out with *Revolutionary Road* and my goat saw so much action that the shy little thing that she is, she needed to withdraw into her pen. With Richard Yates suddenly making a comeback I had to change my old master. So now it is Walker Percy, Yates's old rival and winner of the 1962 National Book Award for *The Moviegoer*. The year as you would remember that Yates made it to the shortlist with *Revolutionary Road* and bought a new dark blue Brooks Brothers suit that he could ill afford. *The Moviegoer*, as too you would remember, is that wildly lyrical novel about a young man of means, drifting about looking for that perfect elusive love. So now with Percy as the default setting, the custom range narrowed to include only *The Moviegoer* and *The Last Gentleman*, these have been months of relative calm but I know soon my goat is going to be terribly restless, bleat a languorous baa and throwing caution to the winds will fuck the first boy with *Atlas Shrugged* by his bedside.

Even though I might ride Zafar ragged through the night and even give his morning chubby a quick parting lick, by the evening I will get all inward and depressed. Once more I have let my goat get the better of me. A good girl should set her standards and stick to them. After all what is there in life if you can't hold on to your own rules. Not for me the man with the gold card or even the big goat. I want the man with the big book. And since I only go out with literary types there is rarely a chance of getting assaulted with a gold card. I want the man who, if he can't write like Auden, has at least read all of Auden. And Dostoevsky, Conrad, Akhmatova, Cummings, Hemingway, Roth and Yevtushenko and when I need to go bhasha on my goat, all of Shakti Chattopadhyay, Kaifi and Shamsher Bahadur Singh.

If then he has a gold card I wouldn't disqualify him. But reading is a must for goat-getting. A reader in my experience makes for a wonderful goat-getter and is the reason why I go for literary types. They are the ones who invariably find without any moral compass the oasis in the desert for my thirsty goat. A man who has travelled with Emma Bovary through her many amours will find my mood swings merely whimsical and not get alarmed when in the morning as Ritwik brushes his teeth, I walk into the bathroom wearing only my rhinestone Alice band, squat on the toilet bowl with my knees drawn up for show and piss like a horse. Rinsing done, I ask him to lick my bottom. I love the smell of Listerine early in the morning. Or 4 a.m. in the morning I wake up John with a gentle tug at his now heartbreakingly vulnerable goat and ask him to leave as I have lain awake for the past hour and must now work on my poem or I will slit my wrists through. Even two strong lines will delay the onset of depression. Just a word would do. Fully formed and transparent as glass, which tugs at my heart with small hands of rain. Don't hug me, don't kiss me, don't make me coffee, just leave dear boy.

Sleeping tucked into the wide shoulders of a good-hearted man is wonderful, his arm warm under my Mao Zedong

T-shirt, gently cupping my breasts. His Gold Flake breath mixed with my goat musk, the stentorian snores and rolling farts make me thank God for giving us men. And keeping me female.

But solitude in its way can be as satisfying as a sweaty legs around the neck half an hour hump. The calm solitude of early winter, after an intensive morning at work, finally worrying the recalcitrant sonnet to submission and then a celebratory gin and tonic in hand, looking at the austere magnificence of the Qutub Minar through my study window. Gives me as much pleasure as tracing my finger from Hriday's pubis up the trail of downy hair to his navel, that is his line of beauty. It is enough to repress my psoriasis for weeks and I can go easy on the cortisone.

A full-grown poem after months, the fallow period finally ends and to celebrate I take my father out to the new mall in Gurgaon. I love its sparkling anonymity and Zed the chance to try out the new boots that I've bought for him from Brent Cross. The kind of desert boots that Richard Yates used to wear with his khaki trousers. He wants to check out the new bookstore on the first floor, to see if they have got Salter's *Light Years*. That is how he judges bookshops. I guess he is his daughter's father. This is how we maintain our standards. At eighty my father is still a magnificent looking man who smells as Annie Haider once coyly remarked 'of morning sunshine mixed with Brut and Amphora Red'. Mother could never stand her. He retains still the craggy, weather-beaten profile with its passing resemblance to Irwin Shaw as printed on the back of his 1989 autobiographical novel about the Progressive Writers' Movement, *Stormy Petrel*. His last. At the mall older women invariably turn and look at him as he passes by. He has resolutely left his walking stick back at home. Women have been doing that to him all his life but he barely notices now. He lost peripheral vision in his left eye due to diabetes a few months back. A huge blow to this man who still likes to look at women in their summer dresses. And Queenie Dhody. He does not find *Light Years* but is not disappointed. He buys for me the collected Ramanujan and for himself a new weekly that has just come out.

In the sea green Ambassador Mark III, returning, suddenly near Chattarpur, flipping the pages of the magazine, he turns to me and says, 'This Arundhati girl really gets my goat.'

'Ah, Zed, you wish,' I say to him and in a flash realize that he has done it again, given me my word of the month. A word that taps on my heart with its small hands of rain. Waiting to be let in.

Father has not heard me. He refuses to wear his earpiece when we go out. Ah, the enduring vanity of the alpha male. He looks at the cover of the magazine and continues, 'This girl is a problem child, just like you.'

His wicked crinkly-eyed smile can still wash away all my despondency in the blink of an eye.

'Ah, baba, I wish.'

Sophia Loren}

Every Sunday morning at about 7 a.m., my father calls me from Patna on the landline. It is a weekly ritual and I have come to depend on it. He never calls me on my mobile phone, nor does he call on any other day except Sunday. Come 7 o'clock and the phone will ring. Without fail. It is a good thing that I am a morning person. He does not even own a mobile phone. His theory is that as it is there is too much communication in the world these days. Too much inconsequential information is exchanged in the name of staying in touch. One shouldn't add to it. Even I am supposed to call on weekdays only if there is something terribly important, otherwise it has to wait till Sunday. 'No phone call means everything is fine. Which is just fine.' Fine. But I know my wife and I would feel a little less worried if my parents did own a mobile phone. They are getting old. 'Hriday, even if something did happen to us, would you be able to reach in time? You live in Delhi. A thousand miles away.' I know even if I did gift him a mobile phone he would keep it switched off. Too much information.

After the usual solicitous enquiry about my health and work, 'How's the bildungsroman coming along?'—he has picked up the word from one of my monthly letters (no e-mails for my father, it has to be handwritten on four sides of a blue inland form), wherein I had mentioned that I was working on an autobiographical novel, a 'bildungsroman'. As a professor of literature he probably likes how the word rolls around on his tongue, the literary glamour, the exotic texture of its sound. He is happy for me—he moves on to news about my extended family, many of whom still live in Patna and also anything significant that happened in our neighbourhood the past week.

After a while my mother comes on the line and usually the first thing she asks me is whether I have had breakfast or not and if I say yes, then I have to tell her exactly what I ate. More often than not I have to invent a large, imaginary breakfast for myself to describe. Who eats breakfast at seven on a Sunday morning? Probably someone who works at a call centre in Gurgaon or Greater Noida and even then it is usually dinner, certainly not breakfast. The breakfast inquisition over, she usually loses interest in me, and demands to speak with my wife. It is a marvel to her that I can survive without her constant supervision even though I have lived away from home for the past thirteen years.

Chitrangada and my mother share a perfect rapport. They are both Sagittarians and have the natural sunny disposition and all-round affability which I believe is de rigueur for that sun sign. They both have great belief in Linda Goodman, Bejan Daruwalla and others of that tribe. But for some strange reason they both read the star sign column of daily newspapers in the evening when the day is usually over. Chitra in the kitchen while making dinner after coming back from her publishing house, where she works as a mid-level marketing executive, and Mother in the drawing room of our Patna house while watching her daily soaps on Zee TV. They both read the predictions more as a gossip column and get quite chuffed when the day promises an 'unexpected romantic encounter'. They never fail to ask each other when they speak on Sundays whether the 'unexpected romantic encounter' on Thursday came true for either of them. Just in case.

Today after handing over the phone to Chitra, I went to the kitchen and started making breakfast. I make passable scrambled eggs with cheese and buttered toast. This is the one meal I cook and enjoy myself doing it. The sense of domesticity and usefulness I feel while breaking five eggs into a medium-sized melamine bowl, then grating couple of cubes of Amul cheese into it, two chopped onions, three chopped chillies, while Dean Martin sings 'I take a lot of pride in what I am' is enormous. It is something that I have inherited from my father, the taste for Italian crooners and I love all of them. Sinatra, Martin and Bennett but more and more as I grow older it is Dean Martin with his bourbon smooth voice and general air of romantic dissolution who does the trick for me each time. One of my earliest childhood memories is of visiting the HMV shop in Hathwa Market with my father to buy an LP of *Christmas with Dino* in the late seventies and later listening to it on our ancient Grundig radiogram. Father rustled up a dinner of French toast with mango pickle. Mother was away visiting my grandparents in Hazaribagh.

I like standing in the kitchen on Sunday mornings like this, as the weak February sun sneaks in bleary eyed through the window and the flat is still drowsy with love, and thinking, 'here, right here, is the centre of my universe.' On a bright sunny day I can even see the Qutub Minar, without putting on my glasses, from the kitchen window. Sometimes in the middle of another hectic day, in my seventh floor office in one of the innumerable high-rises on Tolstoy Marg, where on a good day I might write a quality jingle about Bata shoes (a sight for sore thighs) and MTNL phones (only disconnect!), I think of Sunday mornings and making scrambled eggs with cheese for Chitrangada Thakur. And later taking her out on a drive in my ancient Premier Padmini on the Delhi-Jaipur or Greater Noida expressway, looking for an apartment to invest in in the swish, gated colonies that are coming up on both sides of the highway. If only we had the money. After we have sampled a few 'sample flats', we return late in the afternoon refreshed and at peace with our poverty.

Usually on Sundays I wake up quite early and spend some quality time looking at the sleeping profile of Chitra by my side. I like the way she uses a baby pillow to shade her eyes as the sunlight hits her face through the window curtains that I have just parted. She sleeps like a crumpled floppy soft toy, a luscious Betty Boo, trying to burrow into my body. Some nights trying to burrow deeper she almost gets on top of me. Upon my chest. Maybe she wants a look inside my heart. You are there, darling, you are already there. I gently push her back into the bed. Even after taking a shower I can smell her on my fingers. It will linger throughout the day. My body is the territory she has marked as her own. There is no trail she has left unexplored. Nor any stone unturned. I like being married. I love its everyday voluptuousness and security. This state of round the clock uxoriousness makes me feel incredibly lucky.

Ours was an arranged marriage. According to some of my friends this was a decidedly regressive step. An absolutely unthinkable one for a would-be novelist. That too one who wrote in English. But since this was not London and according to a recent statistic over 80 per cent of marriages in India were still arranged, it was all right. I was in the majority. I would survive. I had fallen in love with a girl while I was in college.

It was quite serious for a while but didn't work out. Then I had gone out with a couple of girls while I was working but it wasn't anything special. I picked Chitra's photograph from the first batch of ten that my mother sent six months into my confirmation as a senior copywriter at a mid-sized advertising agency in Delhi.

In the photograph Chitra was wearing a white T-shirt with denim blue jeans. A black elastic ribbon pulled back her short wedge from her prominent widow's peak. In the background loomed an algae-ravaged water tank with the three stumps of a charcoal wicket clearly marked on it. A sportswoman, no less. There was a bemused expression on her face, as if she were daring me to choose her. I am sure, in the clutch of photographs taken that day by her mother on their Hotshot automatic, there is bound to be one in which Chitra is sticking her tongue out to the world and which her mother has prudently suppressed.

I instantly regretted the photograph I had got of myself clicked at Prem Studio in Kamala Nagar wearing a navy blue pinstripe double-breasted three-piece suit with a with cream-coloured shirt and burgundy tie and which perhaps at this moment Chitra was perusing disdainfully at her residence on Canary Hill Road in Hazaribagh. I had thought of wearing a rented Fedora too but at the last moment my courage gave away.

In retrospect I regret it. It could have been our Bonnie and Clyde moment as both our epithalamic photographs are now framed together and displayed very prominently on the drawing room sideboard.

The next time I was in Patna during Durga Puja, her parents came to meet me, and a month-and-a-half later we got married at her house in Hazaribagh.

I saw Chitra for the first time in the flesh, so to say, during the marriage ceremony itself, during shubho drishti as she very unwillingly hid her eyes with an enormous paan leaf. She had let her hair grow and it now reached her shoulders. I was happy. In fact in all the photographs of the marriage, I have a perennial smile which makes me look as if I were on ganja the whole time. It was noticed by everyone in Chitra's family. In some of the photographs I am smiling even while chanting mantras and the pandit, Bhimsen Chakachak, is looking at me quite quizzically. Chakachak had come down especially from Puri for the wedding. The gouty old bastard later commented to Chitra's mother and aunts that I was the happiest bridegroom he had ever seen in his forty-year career. This after I had given him two bottles of Peter Scot to speed up the marriage ceremony, apart from the regulation dakshina.

The first words that Charu spoke to me early the following morning, while we were sitting down to a breakfast of luchi and aloo-patal and only her younger giggling sisters were around, were, 'God, what were you so happy about? So embarrassing.' Yes, in English, but then she allowed herself a mischievous smile and took a bite of the hot neon-orange imarti. In retaliation I ate two luchis from her plate. And the imarti too.

As soon as the toasts were buttered I carried the breakfast to the dining table. I poured fresh orange juice in two thick-bottomed crystal highballs. The glasses, a set of six with a marvellously tufted decanter in the middle, are the result of a recent celebratory indulgence after a short story of mine was published in the Sunday section of a national newspaper. Two more stories and I will finally have a baker's dozen, enough for a collection. I will be thirty in a month's time and can feel the pressure slowly crawling up my spine. I should have a book out now. Everyone else already has. The 'bildungsroman', unbeknownst to my father, has stalled but the collection is a definite possibility. Chitra wants me to chuck my job and become a full-time writer. I look at the highball and realize that I will never have the courage to do so.

Chitra meanwhile has finished talking on the phone and comes up from behind and hugs me. Beneath the thick flannel dressing gown she is wearing nothing. I can feel it through to my bones. She smells of Sunday. Unwashed and full on sex. I can take her right now on the dining table, like I have done once before. Tad awkward if you must know but doable nevertheless. Only thing, the eggs would get cold. I grip her slender arms and slowly pull her in front of me.

'Love me, please love me,' she implores, her face obscured by her dishevelled hair. I playfully rub her neck from the oesophagus to the chin.

'No, no, not like a dog, Hriday,' she protests.

I make her sit down at the table and serve her.

'So how is Ma?'

'Did you know about this? Do you know what has happened?'

'No, I do not. What are you talking about? What has happened?'

'Sophia Singh is missing from her home. She has eloped with someone from her office.'

'Come on, Chitra, is it again one of your Sophia and me jokes?'

'No, Hriday, this is serious. Ma just told me. She has been missing from her home since Monday. The last anybody saw her was at her bank during lunch time, when she said to one of her colleagues who sat beside her that she was going out to get her sandal repaired. The strap of the right one was actually broken. She never came back. It appears she was having an affair with the new branch manager for quite some time. They were spotted having lunch at Mayfair, you know the restaurant on Fraser Road, a couple of times. The branch manager left soon after but he too never came back.'

'What about her children?' Sophia had two kids, a boy and a girl. The boy was three and the girl five years old.

'They are with the husband. She hasn't taken them with her. The husband has vowed that he will find her and kill them both. Ma thinks that he already has.' Of course she would. The years of endless soap-opera-watching were bound to take their toll one day.

I put the fork down. I had lost my appetite and so had Chitra. Her eyes were full of tears.

When I was thirteen years old, I had fallen in love with Sophia Singh. Only she wasn't called Sophia Singh then, she was known as Sophia Rai. An exotic name for Kadam Kuan, Patna as you could well imagine. Her parents had named her after the famous Italian movie star Sophia Loren, whom they had seen in the movie *Marriage Italian Style*. It was their first movie together, just ten days after they got married. They had driven from Chaibasa to Jamshedpur in the Jonga to see the movie at the Beldih Club in Bistupur. Sophia's father was posted in the Government Hospital, Chaibasa as a general physician. Earlier in the day they had had their first major fight. Sophia's mother was very disappointed with the staff quarters and she let her displeasure be known to her husband. She sat on a small stool in the soot-exhausted kitchen and cried copiously, still dressed in her bridal finery. Daughter of a leading zamindar family of Nawada, no doubt the poky little accommodation was not what she was used to. The movie and the 100-kilometre drive to Jamshedpur and back did much to assuage her hurt and disappointment. Sophia used to tell this story wonderfully. She wanted to see that movie desperately but in the video parlours of Patna, she would never find the videotape.

Sophia and her family had come to Kadam Kuan from Bhagalpur where her father had been posted earlier. They had rented the first floor of the Bannerjee house, on the other side of the children's park. She was two years older and got admission at St Joseph's Convent, where in nine months' time she would take her ICSE Board examinations.

Every evening at about five she would come to our next-door neighbour Mrs Singh for her English and Economics tuition. That was the time when I would be out playing cricket with my best friend Pranjal and other friends on the street. I watched her every day and all of my friends noticed her too. She was pretty in a gangly, stooped sort of way, with a prominent nose and thick shiny black hair down to her shoulders that she would wear in the style of Juhi Chawla in *Qayamat Se Qayamat Tak* which had just been released. She was then an inch taller than me.

About a week later she came over and introduced herself to Pranjal and me. Usually it was just couple of minutes of smiles and chitchat and then one day I asked her for her phone number. 'You are quite forward for a eighth standard boy, aren't you?' she laughed and said, but also passed on her number embedded in the Stephen King novel *Christine* that she had brought for me to read that day. Much later when we were both in Delhi University I would get to know from Pranjal that she had asked him for his number the week before. We had a good laugh about it over a quarter of Old Monk.

'You bastard, all the time you would tag along with us, you were scheming behind my back,' I had said to Pranjal that day.

'Boss, believe me, it was the other way round. You tagged along with us.'

'All right let us call her and find out,' I had said to Pranjal mock seriously.

'Boss, it is three in the morning and she has just got married.' Pranjal as always was the voice of reason. But as any boy who is drunk at 3 a.m. will tell you, the urge to call a girl at that very moment is irresistible. What probably saved her was that it was the early nineties and there were yet no mobile phones. Nor at that time of the night any phone booth open in Kingsway Camp.

'All right, we don't want her to get divorced, Indian style. Do we?' I was quite a bastard those days. I had felt a twinge of jealousy that day when Pranjal had said he too had been in love with her.

It was all very innocent but I still remember the thrill each time I heard her voice over the phone. Perhaps it was not love but something surely very close to it. If she felt anything she never showed it. Sophia was so lively and happy, so full of projects all the time that it would be extremely hard to gauge her true emotions. That she would include me in all her projects was enough for me. But my cousins who lived nearby and friends (Pranjal included, the bastard) would pass meaningful looks every time they saw us speaking. And from there on it had become a family joke, that Hriday was hopelessly in love.

Sometimes on the occasion of some party or festival, Sophia would come over with her parents and we both would be self-conscious that everybody was watching us. I, more than her. Though it was quite embarrassing then, in retrospect I think I quite enjoyed it. Symptoms of love after all—a very grown up affliction, was it not? Over the phone she would mostly talk about her ambitions, her dreams. But then she changed her dreams every other week. From becoming an air hostess one week to being a poet the next one, to a TV quiz show hostess, a police officer, korfball player and so on. But it was always something uncompromisingly glamorous.

Just after her ICSE examination she moved to the flat that her father had bought in Rajendra Nagar. We gradually lost touch after that. She did well in her board examinations and joined Patna Women's College for her intermediate in Arts. And I was still in school. A couple of times a year, I would meet her at various marriages and college and school fairs and during Durga Puja at the Ram Krishna Mission grounds in Nala Road. Every year unfailingly she would call and wish me on my birthday and usually would send a New Year's card. In the evenings she would go to Moinul Haque Stadium for her korfball practice and there I heard she had fallen in love with her coach, who was a Bihar-level player and about fifteen years her elder. It was quite a scandal but since the man, Rajvir Singh, was from the same caste, her parents reluctantly allowed her to marry him.

The last time I saw her was about five years ago during Durga Puja celebrations at Bengali Akhara, a year after her marriage. A heavily pregnant Sophia introduced me to her 'Mister' as a 'special friend' and Rajvir nodded and looked at me with undisguised hostility. I remembered his face from the time, about five years earlier, when he was beaten up by some of my older cousins and their friends in Kadam Kuan during Saraswati Puja. Rajvir had pulled the dupatta of a girl in the pandal. When challenged he had pulled out a revolver and tried to fire it in the air. The revolver jammed. I remember him sitting on the road on his haunches, like he was shitting, with his hands trying to cover his face and head as everybody kicked him. He ran with his one shoe and half of his red-silk shirt still on his back. He was a good athlete all right. For all her glamorous dreams Sophia had married an average mohalla-level lumpen. Later on I got to hear that she had found a junior division clerk's post at Allahabad Bank. For her firstborn's chathi, my mother had visited Sophia's home and she observed after coming back that for a new mother Sophia didn't look that much happy. In a couple of years' time she had a son and after that I didn't have any news of her until this Sunday morning.

As we sat at the dining table and talked about Sophia, I started telling Chitra about all those memories that came rushing to me and some of which I had totally forgotten. Like of the time one New Year's day when she jumped into the lion's enclosure in the Sanjay Gandhi Patna Zoo for a closer look. It was a good thing that the lion, a shy and somewhat reserved individual, had taken shelter inside his mud gufa and was not out ranging the grounds. Sophia in her khaki dungarees was carried out of the moat feet first by two fairly stressed out chowkidars.

In her own feminine way Chitra had intuitively known all along in spite of the jocularity about Sophia and my friendship with her, that it was something that had been important once upon a time, and she felt solidarity with a girl she had never met and who just happened to know her husband when he was a kid.

'She had a pair of black Avis jeans, on the hems of which she had sewn golden stars. She wore them often that year.'

'How does one leave one's marriage and children? How can you leave behind the children?'

'When there is nothing in the marriage, it is better to leave. She couldn't have taken the children with her. If she could she would have. But I do not think she has run off with someone. For once Ma could be right. Sophia would stand her ground. She is what we called 'akkhad'—an evolved form of stubborn. I know right now in Patna, she is being discussed in every home with disgust and a certain malicious pleasure but when I remember her, it is always as a cheerful, slightly flirtatious girl who wanted to shine bright as her name. You know once she and I visited all the video parlours in Patna in a single day to find that movie *Marriage Italian Style*. Couldn't find it. It was her fifteenth birthday and later, still cheerful, she treated me to a double chicken double egg roll at Mayfair.'

The last time I met her, at the Bengali Akhara, when she had introduced me to her 'Mister', she said to me when Rajvir had wandered off towards the exit after pointedly looking at his watch, 'Hriday, since you are in Delhi, do look for that movie that we searched for, all those years ago. I hear in Palika Bazaar one can find anything. You remember the name, don't you? *Marriage Italian Style*. I will pay of course.'

'By the time I reached Delhi after the autumn break, I had forgotten all about it. I never went to Palika to look for it. Never realized that a movie could be so important for someone.'

Chitrangada Thakur reached across and touched my face. Then she rubbed my neck. From the oesophagus to the chin.

'No, not like a dog,' I protested.

We ate our cold breakfast in silence. We hated to waste food.

# Tipple Cake}

I start to worry when Hriday Thakur stops drinking. He is primarily a weekend drinker. Two large pegs of Peter Scot with soda in a tall frosted glass. With three cubes of ice. Every Saturday morning before leaving for work at the Alight Advertising Agency, where he is a senior copywriter now, he will without fail check whether the ice trays have been filled and if not will pour water into them from the tap. When I scold him that he should use the purifier and not the tap, which supplies the rusty brown iron-rich South Delhi water, he points out that Peter Scot is as legendary an antiseptic as Dettol and kills all manner of germs, whether it be physical or mental. I always smile then. He looks forward to his weekend restorative and I take pleasure in his happiness. He used to be a heavy drinker before but not anymore. He puts the ice trays inside the freezer, kisses me on the lips and goes off to work. I then go back to sleep. I work for Proscenium Press and Saturdays are usually off for me.

But for the last two weeks it seems that some mental germs have broken the barrier and have taken prisoner of my Hriday again. He has a propensity for depression and as he only drinks when he is feeling at peace with his world, I am feeling a bit anxious. I am positive, he is unhappy. I like it when he drinks, because it makes him so relaxed and mellow and you can almost hear the whisky hit his bloodstream, drop by drop, as the smile grows larger and conversation more tender. As he is so frugal in his speech otherwise, I welcome the weekend whisky fuelled respite. And later when he mounts me and I wrap my legs around his neck, the whisky on his tongue makes my own rum and Thums Up-breath sweeter.

It all started with the phone call I received from Swastika Singh, couple of weeks back. She wanted us to come for lunch on Sunday and admire the new Anunay Chaubey portrait of Zaheer Abdali that Salim had recently brought back from Patna. I realized later that it was only a ruse. An old university friend of theirs' and Hriday's too, Charulata Roy would also join us. She had recently moved back from Jamshedpur to Delhi after her divorce and had joined a travel portal in Connaught Place as a features editor. She had taken a two-bedroom flat in Model Town near North Campus on rent. Swastika di and Salim of course stayed nearby in Maurice Nagar in Delhi University where Salim had a cosy little flat allotted to him as a Reader in the History Department at the Arts Faculty.

I think at this point in the story it is prudent to mention that Charulata and Hriday have a bit of a history from their university days. I think Hriday wanted to marry her but somehow it never came to pass. Thankfully she left to marry an engineer at Telco in Jamshedpur. So when I informed Hriday about Swastika di's invitation, I thought he would be chuffed to meet an old flame again, but on the contrary I saw a swift flicker of dismay pass over his naturally aloof face and he said, 'not this Sunday, perhaps the next one.' And with that the sabbatical with alcohol and happiness started. Two Sundays have come and gone since then and I quickly became tired with lying to Swastika di about Hriday trying to complete a long story that he was working on for the new book.

I like visiting Salim and Swastika di in their flat in the University. It is a place filled with certain kind of light at all times—a light I associate with the first rays of sun coming out at dawn after a night of rain—which can only come with profound, round the clock love. Even after eight years of being together, the randy buggers can hardly keep their hands off each other.

Their flat is filled with books on history, on politics with an entire rosewood table devoted to Marxism, Hindi, Urdu and English works of fiction and poetry and hundreds of LPs brought from Salim Qureshi's ancestral home at Bihar Sharif. On the walls are oils bought from the Patna and Delhi colleges of art and also Swastika di's small watercolours of the historical monuments of Patna and Delhi. The Gandhi Setu at dawn, the Nizamuddin Dargah in the twilight, Purana Qila by moonlight. Then there is the North Campus series, of St Stephen's College, of Hindu, of Miranda House, of the Gwyer and Jubilee halls and others, of which there is a steady demand through the alumni associations. There is a calmness and at peace with the world quality to her art that exudes instant nostalgia and is very easy on the eye. On our wedding, she had given us two paintings, one of St Xavier's High School in Patna for Hriday and for me one of St Columba's College in Hazaribagh. Both from photographs taken by Hriday. Hriday had taken those photographs with his FM-10, the St Columba's one when he had come to Hazaribagh for our engagement. We had met for the first time then and I had taken him to see my old college in a rickshaw. Ours was an arranged marriage. It took place just before my M.A. [English] results came out. I remember I was more anxious about Spenser and Chaucer than Hriday's thick moustache on my wedding night. I was twenty-three and Hriday twenty-seven. Later I got him to shave off his moustache. It was a definite improvement I feel.

Salim and Swastika had met while they were doing their M.Phil from the History department in D.U. Swastika di is the cousin of Pranjal Sinha. Pranjal and Hriday are childhood friends from St Xavier's, Patna and were roommates in D.U. Swastika di, elder to them by four years, was their local guardian. Pranjal practices as an ophthalmologist in Patna now.

After his M.Phil, while Salim went to King's College, London to do his doctorate on the revenue system of Sher Shah Suri, Swastika di started teaching at Zakir Husain College as an ad-hoc lecturer. After Salim came back from London, they moved in together. Swastika di's mother stopped speaking to her after that, but her father visited her every time he was in Delhi to argue a case in the High Court. Salim's parents, much more progressive than Swastika's, only wished that someday they would legally marry and have children.

Swastika Singh is one of the best looking women I know, with dusky glowing skin, thick shoulder length straight hair, big brown doe eyes with a red bindi in the middle and a long, sharp Rajputani nose which makes her look at times like a calendar art Durga. And Salim Qureshi is the tiger that she uses as her mount, and who is no slouch in the looks department either if you ask me. Not a regulation stunner like Swastika di, he is broadly built, snub nosed with short cropped hair to hide the increasing male pattern baldness and is usually dressed in black twill shirts and blue denim. He looks more like a sculptor than an academic. One of the finest

Marxist historians of his generation, he also edits along with the legendary Samar Sinha, *Hand to Mouth*, a peer reviewed quarterly journal dedicated to history from below. He enjoys the company of women and knows that some women will always find him attractive. Like me for instance, and a few more who still wear Cottage Emporium saris and put big red bindis on their foreheads for target practice. But alas he is totally devoted to Swastika di. I have had a crush on him ever since my marriage to Hriday six years back when I came to Delhi from Hazaribagh. And he has a terrific sense of humour, last year when he wrote an article about lifting the ban on *The Satanic Verses* in *Frontline*, the poor maulanas got agitated and drunk-dialled him to kingdom come, he simply put the Gayatri Mantra as his caller tune. Within twenty-four hours the death threats stopped. 'I always knew the Gayatri Mantra would prove to be more effective than the *Internationale*,' he said.

Over the years I have been accepted into the Delhi University circle that Hriday moves in even though I am much younger. I am now over the years familiar with the legends and landmarks of North Campus and do not feel left out anymore. I have worked hard towards this acceptance into their world of books, of art, of politics and activism. Not to mention, of entitlement, of a sense that what they do is of immediate and immense concern to their country. But the good part is that more often than not they are ironical about their entitlement. Their constant refrain when embarrassed about another good cause to espouse or petition to sign or a party headquarter to picket is a belligerent 'For God and Country'—apparently the old school motto of Salim, Pranjal and Hriday from St Xavier's Patna. They felt blessed that they were young, liberal and left-wing and hoped fervently they wouldn't suddenly turn right-wing and reactionary when they hit forty like their parents. They hoped to keep God at arm's length all their lives.

I enjoy their easy familiarity with drinking or 'tippling' as they call it. The elaborate ritual of it. The ice, the tall glass, the peg measure which after the second peg is always discarded and then the fascinating discourse on the nationalism of drinking, of Old Monk vs Captain Morgan and Peter Scot vs Glenlivet, till the crows wake up.

To tell you the truth nobody has ever imbibed alcohol in my family, at least for the last two generations I am sure. So it was quite a shock for me as I fell in with Hriday's band of merry friends at first. Matal was a word used very liberally by my bhadralok father, when he needed to describe someone he disliked. It was usually used with another epithet—'characterless'. So I found my Hriday to be a 'matal and characterless'. Endearingly so I might add, as soon as I myself discovered a buried thirst for Old Monk and Thums Up. And I loved the conversation lasting all night, as the alcohol flowed and made a tributary of our blood.

I could make out the denial of Peter Scot was totally linked to Charulata Roy. It couldn't be anything else. The work on the new book is finally over and he is doing the last edits before sending it off to Tangent, his publisher. This is his second book, a volume of linked stories and we are both hopeful that it will do better than his first, the short novel *Up North* which got a few glowing reviews but hardly sold at all. So the book couldn't be the reason. Can't be work either as a crisis at the ad agency is a routine affair. No one gets unusually stressed about it. Well there could be one other reason but I do not think Hriday is much bothered by it. At least he has not made it apparent before. For the past five years we have been trying for a baby but no luck so far. We have gone to all the specialists in Delhi and Patna, our mothers to all the gods but no results so far. There is apparently nothing wrong with us. It is just one of those things. Nothing to be done about it.

'We will keep trying.' Hriday flirts with my petite and grey-haired Malayali gynaecologist in Green Park.

'Is there a particular position we should perhaps try?'

'The democratic one always,' she answers stone-faced. It is reassuring to know that he can't charm all women. But this craving for a child does get me down sometimes. The rum helps then. I just go easy on the Thums Up. This six-pound heft of a baby, I constantly carry on my arms like an absence. I love children but Hriday is frankly indifferent to them. 'When I was a child, the thing I hated most was when a grown-up would try to befriend me, thinking I was bored or was in need of company. I liked to be on my own. So I leave kids alone. They too have a right to their privacy.' Hriday can prove to be very strange at times. So it can't be our childlessness. Is it possible that he has still not got over Charulata Roy? Is he still in love with her? Hriday's friends are always a bit vague and offhand when there is a mention of Charulata and I am within striking distance. I have noticed that. Also what sets the minute alarm bells ringing in my heart is that nobody ever joshes Hriday about her like they do about other girls he apparently knew in the past. Which means, I realize with a start that it must have been quite serious at one point in time, not really the oh-so-casual, 'just a girl I was keen on once upon a time' line that Hriday fed me after I discovered a photograph of hers kept between the pages of Zaheer Abdali's

*Stormy Petrel*, three months into our marriage. I am positive now that Charulata Roy is the reason he is trying to dodge Swastika di's invitation. But he can't escape forever.

So this Sunday we finally land up at Swastika di and Salim's home with my signature tipple cake in tow. A full bottle of Sula red had gone into the sponge cake, with raisins soaked in Old Monk, encrusted on the reddish brown crust. This cake of mine is justly famous and Hriday in his wisdom has christened it to be a 'tipple' cake which I think is a vast improvement on the plain old 'tipsy'. A few wedges after dinner with custard, and your night will turn particularly amorous. Swastika di swears by it. But then with Swastika di and Salim bhai even tap water would do the trick.

Salim serves Blue Riband and soda, with freshly squeezed lime and bitters. There is Kalyani Black Label but no one wants the lager. Amonkar sings 'Basant Bahar', in a voice you could carve Rampuri knives out of, in the background. Charulata gives Hriday a quick sideways hug and kisses me on my right cheek. Charulata is accompanied by her son Nihal, who is five years old. She is fairer but not taller than me. Austere looking, with thick shoulder- length hair with natural waves. There are streaks of premature grey at the sides and that surprisingly makes her look younger than she is, like a moustache sometimes makes a man look younger than a clean-shaven face. The introductions are made quickly and Charulata passes on a tall, coolly sweating glass of gin to Hriday, before I can generally caution her that Hriday babu is on a sabbatical. But surprise, surprise, Hriday takes the glass and their hands briefly touch. Noticed that. Hriday picks up Nihal and the delight on his face is something to behold. He puts Nihal on his shoulders and they both go on to admire the new Chaubey. Nihal somewhat startled looks towards his mother. But Charulata only smiles and thus reassured he settles comfortably on Hriday's shoulders, holding on to the head gently. They both look at the portrait of Zaheer 'Zed' Abdali. It is from the famous author photo on the back cover of *Stormy Petrel*, his autobiographical novel of his days with the Progressive Writers' Association. *Stormy Petrel* is one of Hriday's favourite novels. When Salim Qureshi was in the tenth standard at St Xavier's High School in Patna, Zaheer Abdali would come down every Saturday afternoon in his sea green Ambassador Mark III to teach an hour-long class on writing short stories, with a lit pipe smouldering continuously between his lips. It was only for six months but Zaheer Abdali's writing, personality and political views would influence him very heavily. In Delhi University Salim would join the CPI-ML and become a card carrying member like Abdali. On the other hand Zaheer Abdali's daughter Sadaf would teach Hriday at the Arts Faculty while he was doing his M.A. (Final) in English.

'He looks like Irwin Shaw here, like in the famous Capa portrait.' Hriday says to Salim and Swastika, who have come to join him and Nihal. I slice some more lemons and look over to Charulata. She in turn is watching me. She smiles and takes a small sip of the gin fizz which the bitters have turned pink and walks over to look at the painting closely.

'He was better looking than Shaw, I once saw him read at Zakir. The women couldn't keep their eyes off him. Men too. He was over seventy then but still magnetic. Sadaf led him up to the dais. He read his soon to be a classic "Butcher Out of Gujarat". It was just after the riots,' Sawastika di said to Hriday.

'A much better writer than Shaw too, if you ask me.' Salim took a sip of his gin fizz.

'True but Shaw wrote some wonderful stories. "The Eighty-Yard Run" is magical,' Hriday pointed out.

'And not to forget "Girls in their Summer Dresses". Hriday once read that story to me long back. Just before the Ancient India paper in M.A. (Previous) to calm me down. I was so nervous. Do you remember Hriday?' Charulata poured some more Blue Riband into her glass and said softly.

'Of course, I remember.' Hriday put Nihal down gently on to the sofa and lit a Gold Flake.

To calm her down! Really Hriday babu. But then it does seem to be in character. Hriday is a gallant lad, if anything. But I am sure Hriday wouldn't just stop at the reading. He would then have really *calmed* her down. Even if it took him all night. With friends like these, it is a miracle Charulata could clear her masters in history.

A cloud seemed to have lifted off Hriday and he took Nihal by the hand and went over to the small ox-blood chesterfield by the Grundig. And they kept talking, completely absorbed in each other's company. Nihal told him stories of the school he went to in Jamshedpur called 'Lilies of the Field'—more like 'Brood of Vipers' Charulata interjected—and about all his friends. The gin and lime went down like water in the drowsy February afternoon and before lunch Hriday already had three large ones. But he was absolutely fine. He was back in character, the despondency had slid off him like a cloak. And it was a relief to see him imbibe and enjoy himself once more. With four large gin and limes, I wasn't doing badly either. From the corner Suzanne Vega reiterated that 'Blood Makes Noise'.

At the dinner table I sat with Charulata on my left and Swastika di on the right. On the opposite side, sat the boys, with Nihal between Salim and Hriday eating macaroni and cheese quite adroitly off his fork. While I had cold pepper chicken in white sauce, Hriday had broiled bhetki with a liberal spread of Colman's mustard. According to Salim, Colman's mustard was the one thing that someone called Philby dearly missed in Moscow.

Even though I knew I would have a raging hangover in the evening, it was a wonderful, languid late February lunch and we all felt happy and privileged. As it invariably happens in such gatherings, after a certain point we started talking about caste and privilege and how lucky we were to be born in the kind of families we were born into. Then Charulata narrated an incident that happened while she was coming to Swastika di's house in an autorickshaw. 'At the Kingsway Camp traffic lights, as the auto stopped, a little girl not more than five years old, with a baby in her arms came and touched my arm. She looked as if she hadn't had a meal in days. My heart went out to her. I gave her ten rupees. And this keeps happening at every traffic signal in Delhi. It wasn't so earlier.'

'It was always there. They are all from Bihar, Jharkhand, Orissa and Chhattisgarh, caught between the Maoists and the government forces,' Salim said to Charulata.

'Well, the poor will always be with us,' Swastika di said and filled her glass with the Chardonnay that Charulata had brought as hostess present.

'It is a shame. I have been thinking of writing a short story about the child beggars of metropolitan India for a long time,' Hriday said to Salim.

'It is all very well organized. They earn quite a lot. The

contractors, that is. You should never give them money. It is taken away from them by the contractors. It is all futile,' I said to Charulata.

Charulata looked at me for a moment and then said, 'Chitrangada, it is hard not to, when you are a mother.' I felt as if she had leaned across and thrown a glass of cold Chardonnay into my face. I felt so ashamed and judged. And then angry at Hriday. He should have said something but he didn't. He played the perfect gentleman. He kept quiet and then tried to change the topic by asking Nihal if he would like some more macaroni. I poured myself some more Blue Riband. Salim got up and brought me some ice and refreshed his own drink. The conversation drifted away. Why did Charulata have to say something so cruel to me? I had liked her, and whatever there had been once between her and Hriday, I was willing to overlook. I could see that Hriday was still affected by her presence but not so much that it would affect our marriage. But what really struck me was the instant bond that Hriday had forged with Nihal. The open pleasure he took in Nihal's company. I realized with a jolt that Hriday probably wanted a child as much as I did. Today his mask had slipped.

After my tipple cake and custard were served, we left. There was ice cream and gulab jamuns for Nihal. Swastika di filled a square Tupperware box with slices of the tipple cake for me to take home, as Hriday and I hadn't eaten any at the table.

On our way back, at the Kingsway Camp traffic signal, I felt the first stirrings of the slowly creeping hangover and saw the light-orange matinee sun making everything hazy, as some child beggars went from one indifferent car to another with their hands outstretched. Before Hriday could stop me,

I was out on the streets carrying the box of cake in my hands, calling out to the kids. Some people in the neighbouring cars rolled down their windows and looked at me in wonder. The children with their emaciated and malnourished bodies and hair bleached blond by the sun, hesitated for a bit and then ran over. Just as I opened the Tupperware box and started passing the pieces of cake lovingly to them, Hriday came from behind and snatched the cake pieces back from the hands of the startled children. I hit him from the back, on his shoulders then but Hriday pretended not to notice. Still busy playing the gentleman. He took out of his pocket whatever loose change he had and now gave it to the tiny beggars. They ran shrieking, throwing their hands in the air. The light turned green and Hriday took me by the hand firmly and opened the car door. He helped me put the seat belt on, then smiled and had a slice of the tipple cake. He gently wiped the tears from my eyes with his fingers, rubbed my chin playfully like a pet dog's and we drove back home.

# Death of a Proofreader}

At the funeral of Samuel Aldington Macauley Crown, in the old Paharganj cemetery, six people besides the priest of St James' Church were present by his graveside. His wife Joyce Crown, in a pale yellow and green cotton sari; his boss the redoubtable Jehangir 'George' Tekari sweating prodigiously in a khaki-coloured seersucker suit; a light-blue Oxford shirt and black tie; his young colleague Hriday Thakur in black jeans, thick-soled Kolhapuri chappals and a white khadi kurta; Roshan Lal, the neighbourhood beggar; Imogen Burns, a young Scottish historian from Edinburgh working on colonial era cemeteries in north India, who had wandered in by chance; and Dudley Brown, long-time friend and pianist at the Maypole Club, in black trousers and white shirt, with the sleeves half rolled.

If S.A.M. Crown had lived a little longer, say for a couple of years more, he would surely have worked on Imogen's book, because for the past quarter century or so, by his own admission no less, Crown was the best proofreader in all of Ansari Road.

Ansari Road, Daryaganj, as you would know, is the book district of New Delhi and all of India by association. All the major publishers or their distributors have their offices here. Flanked on one side by an old historic wall of the Delhi Gate through which the British entered in 1858 to reclaim the besieged old town and on the other by the Ring Road and the Rajghat and Shantivan bus stops, on most mornings between eight and nine you can see a myriad editors, proofreaders and book salesmen who ply their trade on that street make their way to the various publishing houses. Oxford, Macmillan, UBS, Rupa, Cambridge, Manohar, Tangent, Proscenium and hundreds of others.

Samuel Crown was born just before India got independence, at the railway hospital in Mughalsarai to an Anglo-Indian father who was an engine driver and a Bihari Protestant mother from Bettiah. His great grandfather had been a printer from Stirling in Scotland, who ran a small print shop near the Allahabad High Court in the post-Mutiny years. He had married a Pathan widow, whose husband had been killed at the siege on the Lucknow Residency in 1857. By the time of Samuel Crown, who was very dark and of short stature, the vestige of Scottish inheritance that remained locked in his DNA was his intense love of whisky. He would imbibe copious amounts each night before staggering off to have his dinner at one of the many street-side eateries around the Paharganj railway station. That night, the Christmas Eve of 1998, he had decided to grace the august precincts of Yadavji Litti Centre and have their fabled Patna Large. Four pieces of litties (two of which he would pass on to the beggar Roshan Lal, an old acquaintance and a habitué of the pavements), two pieces of mutton in a fiery red curry and brinjal and potato chokha. It would be here on that fateful night that Hriday Thakur would first meet Crown, intrigued by the sight of a fifty-something gentleman, wearing a blue travel blazer with gold buttons, steel grey immaculately pressed worsted trousers and dark tan brogues, reading a Penguin paperback of

*A Tale of Two Cities* and eating litti-chokha, seated on a black wooden bench with a beggar wrapped in a patched multi-coloured Indian Railways blanket for company. A long thin black umbrella with a curved handle was propped against the table. There had been rains.

Hriday Thakur was then at a low point in his life. He was in his early twenties, a Bengali-speaking Bihari from Patna, who had abandoned his M.Phil in Shakespeare Studies from Delhi University midway and was now trying to write a novel. An ambition he had nursed assiduously from childhood. He had also, the night he met Crown, just been fired from his first job. The position had been that of a subeditor with a lifestyle magazine called *Touch*, which was published from a couple of rooms near Shivaji Stadium. His mandate had been to write soft-porn short stories and he felt he was doing quite well until that afternoon when he was tragically let go. To celebrate the debacle he had imbibed a good amount of whisky that evening and was now ravenous. As a thunderclap exploded over Paharganj, Hriday hailed Yadav at the counter and ordered a Patna Large.

'Dear boy, is that a genuine Harris Tweed jacket that you are wearing or is it only my old Scottish eyes playing up tricks on the native plains?' Crown bellowed across the table unnecessarily, as Hriday took his seat alongside Roshan Lal.

'It is Harris Tweed all right, dear sir. You can still smell the Outer Hebrides on its weave when it rains, even though it is over fifty years old,' Hriday Thakur bellowed back, affecting an impromptu Connery brogue.

'I do not want to smell you, dear boy, as I am not a devotee of the metre gauge but I will take your word that it is a Harris Tweed. Certainly looks the same. Do you know the

Scots used to wear it to battle?'

'Not really, but I am sure you are right. A good Harris Tweed coat does straighten your back and lend your posture a martial air.'

'A highlander is always ready for battle. S.A.M. Crown at your service, sir. My forefathers came down from Bridge of Allan near Stirling to provide culture to the natives. I am continuing the same. I am senior proofreader with Proscenium Press, purveyors of quality monographs in the social sciences. A book a week.'

Crown proffered his surprisingly large, thick-fingered hand to Hriday across the table and Hriday gladly shook it.

'I too harbour ambitions in that very trade. Hriday Thakur's the name and writing is my game. As they say. This is a most fortuitous meeting, I am sure.'

'Published or unpublished?'

'Still a virgin, sir. Entirely unpublished.'

'Then you shouldn't call yourself a writer yet. At least two published books before you start introducing yourself as one. That's the rule.'

'Isn't that a bit elitist? What about Kolatkar?'

'Of course, but it is needed. All games must have rules. As for Kolatkar, he doesn't count. He is a genius. I compared the first proofs of *Jejuri* for Shahane in a day.'

'Well, if you insist. I am working on my first novel and for the past few weeks was a copyeditor with a lifestyle magazine in Connaught Place. I resigned some hours back. I am a free bird again.'

'Which skin rag was it?'

'*Touch*.'

'A *Touch* of class. Of course,' Crown laughed and then

choked on a bit of litti and Roshan Lal reached across to thump him on his back.

Meanwhile Yadav brought over Hriday's order of Patna Large. And then over litti and Dickens, in the late December chill, Crown and Hriday bonded and a friendship was forged.

Hriday talked about literature, his ambition to be a published writer one day, to see his name on the spine of a Faber and Faber hardback, about his family in Patna, and his years as a literature student in Delhi University's North Campus. Crown knew some of the teachers who had taught Hriday at the Arts Faculty, many of whose books he had seen through the press over the years at different houses. The great D.W. Sardesai, with his perpetually torn at the shoulders and totally relaxed brown houndstooth jacket, Angika Paul with the hibiscus in her hair, the brilliant and very young Sadaf Khan Abdali, daughter of the legendary Zed, the affable Harish Trivedi from Allahabad and the Marxist Badri Raina—who bore a striking resemblance to Salman Rushdie with his full salt-and-pepper beard and receding hairline—whose tutorials of *Dombey and Son* were legendary. And then Crown talked about his family. His wife Joyce Barnali Shaw, who was his second cousin from Danapore Cantt near Patna and with whom he had fallen in love thirty years ago at the wedding of an aunt in Meerut. A month after that he had visited Patna and Joyce had eloped with him. 'She met me outside the front gates of the Patna Women's College clutching a small British Airways shoulder bag with one yellow and green sari and a Bible in it.' They were married at the St James' Church in Kashmere Gate a week from the day they reached New Delhi. They started their married life in Crown's cosy two-room rented apartment in Multani Dhanda near Paharganj. Crown was then working for Gulab Vazirani in the production department of Arnold Heinemann. Their married life was very happy and a few years later they were blessed with a baby girl, whom they named Portia. On the day Portia was born, Crown was appointed as senior proofreader by Oxford University Press, at its Ansari Road office, under the legendary Surya Mathur.

'There couldn't ever be another Surya Mathur in Indian publishing. I learnt all there was to learn about proofreading sitting at his feet. He could at a glance tell you that the space between an A level and text was off by 2 picas. An austere man, smoking bidis, he would serve scotch to his guests while drinking Peter Scot himself. I still occasionally do proofreading for him. He has his own publishing house now. He only publishes fiction. I could introduce you, if you wanted.'

'Peter Scot is a good whisky. Government-approved,' Hriday replied.

'I am sure it is! I could smell it off you a mile back. How many pegs did you take down?'

'Four or five. A friend was buying. At Volga.'

'I can't afford to drink Peter Scot. My choice of amrit is Bagpiper Gold. I love the name. Reminds me of the Highlands.'

'Bagpiper is fine too,' Hriday concurred.

As the coffin was lowered into the grave, Joyce Barnali Crown read from W.B. Yeats: 'The Lake Isle of Innisfree'.

*I will arise and go now and go to Innisfree*

Then it was Hriday's turn and he read from Crown's own copy of *A Tale of Two Cities*, the justly famous first paragraph which Crown used to love and declaim at will after a quarter bottle of Bagpiper.

Imogen just threw in a handful of earth into the grave and stepped back. From the station the long wail of the Rewari Passenger could be heard.

As the service ended Hriday went over to Joyce Crown, who was talking with Dudley Brown, and said, 'Samuel was a wonderful man. He helped me and got me a job when I was in a very bad state.' She nodded and turned and walked away towards the front gate, closely followed by Dudley.

'Shall we go off to the office?' Hriday's boss, Jehangir 'George' Tekari asked him, taking off the drenched jacket. Jehangir got the name George from Crown because of his addiction to John le Carré's George Smiley novels and his firm belief that publishing was just like spying, it attracted the same kind of talent and Proscenium Press was the 'Circus' and Oxford University Press 'Moscow Centre'. He called his vast network of freelance copyeditors 'lamp-lighters' and insisted on 'Moscow Rules' while dealing with them. Hriday liked him very much.

'I think I will take the day off, George, if it is all right. Don't have the courage to enforce the style on a recalcitrant bibliography today. No ibids, no op.cits, no more idems either. I will walk back to my room after a while. You can take the priest back to St James if he wants to leave.'

'Make sure you are not followed. Or de-briefed against your will,' George Tekari advised Hriday looking pointedly at Imogen Burns. He then lit a Charminar with a gold Dunhill lighter and walked over to the priest who was giving some instructions to Samson the gravedigger.

'*A Tale of Two Cities*. Isn't that an odd thing to read at a funeral?' Imogen Burns said to Hriday as they watched

Samson fill the grave.

'Did you know him well?' Hriday asked her, looking at Imogen's long, damp blond hair, which she wore parted at the centre like Joni Mitchell.

'I do not even know his name.'

'Samuel Aldington Macauley Crown. Proofreader extraordinaire.'

'I saw the service and stopped by. I am working on a monograph on colonial era cemeteries and tombstones. I meant no disrespect, about *A Tale of Two Cities.* Imogen Burns.'

Hriday shook her soft, surprisingly dry, small-boned right hand and said, 'That was Crown's favourite novel. He thought of himself as a born again Sidney Carton. Hriday Thakur.'

After that fateful meeting at Yadavji Litti Centre, Hriday and Crown parted ways, Crown carrying on to Kashmere Gate for the midnight service at St James' Church and Hriday back to his room at Hotel Kama in Paharganj. Crown had asked Hriday to meet him at his office in Proscenium Press after Christmas. He promised he would find him a job on the copy desk. But when on Christmas day Hriday woke up around noon, the previous day's memory was quite hazy with regard to S.A.M. Crown and their intense whisky-fuelled conversation. To atone for his previous day's dissipation, Hriday worked on his novel for the next three days, surviving only on bread, jam and tea. In the morning and in the evening he did his usual hundred push-ups in sets of fifty. Once on the second day he went out for bananas and Gold Flake and to deposit a cheque for 350 rupees at the SBI branch across the road. He finished about two chapters and by the end of the third day had written over 5,000 words. That gave him an adrenalin rush and he felt elated enough to venture out of his room and walk to Connaught Place. By the side of the Paharganj cemetery he bought a single Dunhill cigarette for three rupees and lit it from an evenly smouldering jute rope kept for the purpose. There was a hole-in-the-wall second-hand bookshop near Plaza cinema, where Hriday hoped to find a John D. MacDonald-Travis McGee novel for twenty rupees. By this time he had totally forgotten the name of the house that Crown worked in and even if he had remembered he probably wouldn't have kept his appointment regarding a position there. When not in his cups, Hriday Thakur was a very shy young man who got embarrassed at the most trivial of events. At the Plaza bookshop, Hriday feeling splendid after a brisk twenty-minute walk, with almost a week's work done in his notebook, browsed to his heart's content. Even though he didn't find a Travis McGee novel, he found to his delight a brand new copy of the Ross Macdonald-Lew Archer novel, *The Goodbye Look*, and the Tangent edition of Zed Abdali's cult classic, *Stormy Petrel.* He also found Dalton Trumbo's classic tract against the Communist witch-hunt in America, *The Time of the Toad.* He had learned about it in Navasky's *Naming Names*, which he had read sitting in the Central Reference Library at the Arts Faculty while he was doing his M.Phil course work. He haggled vigorously with the bookseller and paid 150 rupees for the three books. He felt this was God's way of rewarding him for putting in 5,000 words over the last three days.

He suddenly felt very hungry and started walking towards Keventer's with the intention of gorging on their oversized vegetable patties and a bottle of strawberry-flavoured milk.

Thus fortified he would call up his parents and inform them about the sad demise of his first job. He had been putting it off. But as he came out of the subway near Regal Cinema, he found S.A.M. Crown right in front of him trying on a second-hand navy blue blazer, standing on the busy pavement, a clutch of similar blazers lying in a heap at his feet. Before Hriday could make a quick about-turn and flee into the subway, Crown bellowed his name, startling the rotund coat-seller who was trying to button up Crown's blazer.

'Ah, Mr. Crown, how are you, sir?'

'Hriday Thakur, you are a strange bird. Yes, you are. I waited for you at Proscenium for three days. I had spoken to Mr Tekari, our editor-in-chief, for a position on the copy desk. But of course, you didn't turn up. Do you want a job or not?'

'Yes, I do, Mr Crown. I was very ill. I had a stomach flu. Couldn't move out of my room for three days. Was on a liquid diet. I will come to your office tomorrow.'

'Well, excellent. There is the small matter of a copy test that you need to pass. I hope you won't mind. It is mandatory.'

'No, of course not. In life there is always a copy test.'

'Oh, you will clear it with flying colours. A man who is a friend of Sidney Carton, as you are, has no cause for worry.' Crown removed the blazer he was trying out and picked up his own from the pile at his feet, searched through the pockets and found a packet of Charms and offered one to Hriday. Crown lit a cigarette and said to the coat-seller, 'Too tight. Find a hunting jacket for me, Chaddha, will you? Leather elbow patches and extra-large pockets for cartridges. Preferably Abercrombie & Fitch.'

'Are you going hunting, Crown Sahab? I will look for one.

Come next week,' the coat-seller said to Crown as Hriday and he started to walk towards Mohan Singh Place.

'Hemingway always used to wear one. A hunting jacket with extra-large pockets.'

'But instead of cartridges, in mine there will be books and an addha of Bagpiper Gold. A bottle of which I must absolutely buy before heading home. Good call about Hemingway, though, you must have read the Lillian Ross profile. I was only showing off. I have similarly placed orders for a Barbour waxed jacket, a Burberry trench coat, a Brooks Brothers topcoat and a Savile Row tuxedo. He is yet to find me any, of course.'

There was a theka in the back alley behind Mohan Singh Place and from there Crown made his purchase of Bagpiper Gold.

'Would you like to visit my room and see the Crown Jewels, Hriday Thakur?'

'So he was gay after all? Imogen said to Hriday as they sat on a slatted wooden bench under a peepal tree in the cemetery, smoking Gold Flakes in the intense and humid late-May Delhi heat. They were waiting for some photostats of the burial records from colonial times. Hriday had a wet white cotton towel wrapped around his neck and Imogen was wearing a floppy olive green-coloured canvas hat, the brim and sides of which were sopping wet with sweat. She sipped regularly from a litre bottle of mineral water kept by her side. The green wooden bench on which they sat said it had been donated in 1989 by Mrs Rose Cowell in memory of her husband Dr Stuart Cowell, veterinary surgeon, Meerut Cantt. Hriday watched a thin stream of sweat travel from Imogen's red inflamed throat to the valley of her ample cleavage. Caught checking out her breasts, he smiled and pointed to the bottle of mineral water. Imogen passed it to him and Hriday took a long draught, tilting his head and keeping the bottle an inch away from his mouth. Imogen watched him with fascination and then said softly, 'I wouldn't mind if you put your lips to it.'

'I would,' said Hriday in equally soft tones and put the dark blue cap back on the bottle. In a flash it came to him that he didn't know the English equivalent of jootha. He ought to know it, after all he was supposed to be a writer. But he didn't. Perhaps there was no such word. Contamination didn't quite convey the same meaning. Neither did taint or spoil. Perhaps jootha was a particularly Indian concept that no other culture followed. Not even Indian, it was singularly Hindu, its policies honed razor-sharp to cut-throat perfection, drawing blood at merest glance, at any interaction between man and man. Segregation after all was at the heart of the Hindu way of life. And because of that India wouldn't ever be united but on the other hand nor would it ever splinter. Caste and community would see to it that there was no consensus ever. Whether of the left-wing or the right-wing variety. Even though his thirst was sated, Hriday took another sip of the bottle, pressing it gently to his lips this time.

Crown unlocked the door of his second floor flat in a gali off Multani Dhanda and switched on the tube light by the side of the door. Hriday crossed the threshold and took in Crown's habitat with a novelist's, or rather a naturalist's, dispassionate gaze. It was a flat not more than 400 sq. ft., with a largish sitting room, wooden cane shelves all around stacked with books, two rosewood almirahs with glass doors containing nothing but books, a large sheesham writing table with two wooden high-backed chairs with armrests and in the corner a two-seater red leatherite sofa. There was a small folding table under the window, which had a view of the children's park downstairs, on which were arrayed a small 5-kg gas cylinder, a one-burner Prestige steel stove and a magnificent brass samovar, which had a detail of Russian women dancing amidst closely packed haystacks. The samovar held Hriday's attention.

'For years I had proofread *Soviet Woman* and *Soviet Darpan* for the Russians. In 1989 just before the wall came down, they took me on a two-week tour of Russia. I visited all the big publishers, Pravda, Progress, Raduga. I bought the samovar in Leningrad, off the Nevsky Prospect metro station, walking back from the Pushkin Museum by the side of the Moyka River.'

There was a small white-coloured Kelvinator fridge in one corner. There was no TV anywhere but on the writing table was kept a small Bush record player and a stack of long playing records, mostly crooners, Nat King Cole, Frank Sinatra, Jim Reeves, Tony Bennett, Dean Martin and Rosemary Clooney. In the corridor which connected to the bedroom at the back, there was a washbasin with a mirror. The bedroom had a wooden folding cot and another small table with more books on it. On it was also kept a Corona 3 typewriter—'Hemingway used one to compose his lost stories'—and a coffee cup full of pencils, regular, blue and red-nibbed; some manuscripts and proofs for comparing and a bottle of Kores whitener. This was his proofreading table. There was a wooden chair with plastic weaving.

There was a small bathroom with a commode and a shower

to one side. There was no door to it but a thick plastic black-and-red shower curtain you pulled when you went to take a piss. The odd thing was there was no evidence of women in the flat; surely, Hriday thought, Crown had mentioned a wife and a daughter that night while they were having litties over Dickens.

Crown came up behind Hriday, put his hand on his shoulder and pointed to the stack of books kept within two swan-shaped bookends on the table.

'Those, Hriday Thakur, are the Crown jewels.'

'Those books?'

'Yes, five of them. One more precious than the other.'

Crown picked up each book and showed them to Hriday, opening each at the title page so that he could read the inscription.

'*The Elements of Style* by Strunk and White, given to me by Samuel Israel when I was at Macmillan in the early seventies. *Hart's Rules for Compositors* presented to me by Surya Mathur on the day I completed a month at Oxford University Press. It has his proofreading marks on some pages, where he had found faults with word-breaks and leading. The *Chicago Manual of Style*, look at the inscription "From an Unknown Cricketer to a Master Proofreader". Sujit Mukherjee gave his old copy to me on my farewell at Orient Longman. This is perfect for American books. *Copy-editing* by Judith Butcher. This was given to me by Bhola Varma at Manohar when the new edition came up. I have freelanced for him for a long time. And this, the Viking edition of *The Portable Kipling* was given to me by Zameer Ansari at Penguin when I read the first proofs of *A Suitable Boy* in three weeks. All 1500 pages of it.'

All the volumes, effusively inscribed by these legends

of Indian publishing, were testimony to the singular talent and 'hawk-like eyes' (Surya Mathur) of Samuel Aldington Macauley Crown. They went back to the front room and Hriday took in the books in the almirahs and shelves. By that time Dudley Brown, Crown's pianist friend and drinking partner, had joined them and was pouring water out of the samovar. The books were mostly nineteenth century and early twentieth century modern English literature. Dickens, Hardy, Thackeray, Gissing, Stevenson, Walter Scott, Kipling, Yeats, Byron, Swinburne, Auden, Housman, Walter de la Mare and P.G. Wodehouse. Of the Americans, there was Hemingway, Fitzgerald, Hammett and the complete stories of Irwin Shaw. Narayan, Desai, the early bright Naipauls, Rushdie's *Midnight's* represented the Indians. And of course Vikram Seth's *A Suitable Boy*, playfully inscribed by the author on the title page.

*For*
*The unsinkable Mr. Samuel Crown*
*Who with nary a frown*
*Rose up through the words*
*Alas never to drown.*

Hriday felt a special thrill while reading the inscription as Seth too was a Patna boy and a Xaverian to boot, like him.

Crown obviously read a lot, as he told Hriday, this was his university; he had never gone to college. He was only a matriculate from the Railway High School, Mughalsarai. He had come to Delhi at the age of fifteen and had joined the Liddle Press in Paharganj as an apprentice compositor and had learnt all about printing in the five years he spent there. Among the fonts, Baskerville, Sabon and Goudy Old Style were his favourites. He would set up the type by hand, row upon careful row, make up the slug matter, check the galleys and learn all about leading and breathing the text. By the end of the second year, old man Liddle even trusted Crown to make the final corrections before the formes went to the machine room. In the evenings he would read and get an education. Poor and naturally street smart, he would also now acquire sophistication beyond his class. The first thing he did was to start speaking in English that was wholly picked up from the Wodehouse countryside. That opened quite a few doors for him. He felt a kinship with his Scottish heritage and wanted to visit Scotland, especially Stirling where his great grandfather was born. He wanted to check whether his stone cottage by the side of Allan Water was still standing. He started paying attention to his clothes and would turn out in immaculate fashion for his job at the press, much to the amusement of old Mr Liddle in his baggy khaki shorts made by the same tailor in Jhandewalan who catered to the shakha nearby. Crown would turn up in a white or light blue cotton shirt with steel grey or khaki trousers in the summer and a navy blazer in winters. On his feet were dark-tan brogues with white socks. This uniform which he attained at the age of nineteen and would never forgo was picked up from his hero Salim Durrani, whom he saw one evening at the Maypole Club in Connaught Place sipping Golden Eagle beer standing beside the piano, surrounded by adoring matrons. Durrani, out of the national team yet again, was in Delhi to play an exhibition match at the Roshanara grounds.

Crown used to sing in the church choir in Mughalsarai and had a strong mellifluous voice and he added Nat King Cole, Sinatra and Dean Martin to his repertoire. He would be asked to sing at the Maypole Club and there one day after he had just finished singing 'Nature Boy' with the band, he had a most fortunate meeting with Ned O'Toole of Oxford University Press, who would recommend him to his friend Gulab Vazirani at Arnold Heinemann and thus Crown entered the world of publishing.

'This is how it works in publishing. O'Toole thought my rendition of Nat King Cole was eccentric enough to recommend me for a job and now your Harris Tweed coat will get you a seat at Proscenium.'

Crown promised and that is exactly how it happened the next day after Hriday took the mandatory copy test. Proscenium was a left of centre publisher and specialized in monographs on South Asia. The owner, a rich, oncologist cousin of George Tekari, lived in Austin, Texas. Hriday was given a desk and chair outside of George Tekari's office and for the first couple of days he catalogued the huge pile of manuscripts which graced the large steel Godrej almirah that was kept near the windows in Mr Tekari's cabin. After that he started with tallying first and second proofs of a volume on the Hungry Movement poets of the 1960s. The movement started by two brothers from Patna—Malay and Samar Roy Chowdhury—would radically change the pitch of Bengali poetry. The volume made for fascinating reading as a substantial part of it was set in Patna and dealt with the early years and influences of the brothers Roy Chowdhury. The volume, by a young American couple, disciples of A.K. Ramanujan, was being done in partnership with the Chicago University Press. Around 3 o'clock each afternoon, Mr Tekari would invite Hriday into his office and give him a sack full of review copies to take to newspaper and magazine offices.

'Do not leave the books at the reception. Always meet the book reviews editor. Make personal contact. Become their friend. Recruit them to the cause. That is field craft.' Hriday liked those trips. Some of the offices were nearby, *The Times of India*, *Pioneer*, *Indian Express*, *Business Standard*; *Hindustan Times* and *India Today*, a little further in Connaught Place, near Volga, where afterwards Hriday would stop by for a large glass of their draught beer. And then continue on to *The Hindu* in the INA building on Rafi Marg. The review editors were a few years older than Hriday and some were poets and writers of fiction and quickly Hriday made many friends among them. There were others too far away like *The Asian Age* in South Ex and *Outlook* in Safdarjung Enclave. But most days he was free of his chores by 5.30 in the evening. His salary was now 8,000 rupees and he got two formal trousers, one black and one steel grey, made by Crown's tailor in Jhandewalan, to be paid for at the start of the next month. He also bought a clutch of white shirts and he was all set to storm the publishing world. He already had the Harris Tweed coat. His parents in Patna were relieved and happy for him. Hriday liked his work and by the end of the month George Tekari even trusted him to do some line edits on a history volume by the noted subalternist Samar Sinha. Samar Sinha of course was married to Mira Verma, the novelist, whom Hriday had met long back with Ritwik Ray, his writer friend from Patna. According to George Tekari, who was a friend of Samar Sinha from his Gwyer Hall days in Delhi University, Samar and Mira were now separated and Mira, at that point of time, was based in Dhanbad working on a volume on the great trade union leaders of post-independence India. She was in Dhanbad to interview A.K. Roy of the Marxist Coordination Committee

(MCC) and then she would go to Raipur in Madhya Pradesh to research the life of Shankar Guha Niyogi, who was shot dead by an industrial cartel in 1988. Already she had spent over a month in Jamshedpur for her profile of the legendary Gopal, of Tata Steel, who was killed in 1990.

The volume *Red Harvest: Trade Unionism in Independent India 1947-2000* would be published in Spring 2001 to strong reviews. *Economic and Political Weekly* of Bombay would call it 'trenchant' and an 'eye opener'. *Biblio* would, in a review essay entitled 'Profiles in Courage' by the novelist Anjali Nalwa, call it a classic study of how upper-caste liberal democracy feeds off the downtrodden and poor with its skewed economic policies. This would also be the last book that Hriday would copyedit and see through the press before going on to join advertising via a short detour in academia. The pay was much better there. But all this was in the future. In the five months before his death from a massive heart attack Crown taught Hriday as much about the technical side of publishing as he could grasp. Most evenings after work they would catch the same bus for Karol Bagh, from the Golcha Cinema Hall bus stand in Daryaganj. Hriday would get down at Paharganj, Crown continuing onwards for a few more stops.

Crown's marriage had broken up in the early 1990s over his drinking. His wife now lived with her brother in Dilshad Garden and taught English at a Kendriya Vidayalya near Pitampura. The divorce had been amicable to some extent and Joyce met Crown every Sunday morning at St James' Church in Kashmere Gate and provided him news about Portia, who was now in Australia doing a course in Hospital Management. Portia didn't keep in touch with Crown as she blamed him entirely for her parents' shattered marriage. 'She is right, you know,' Crown would say, acknowledging the enormity of his folly in letting the marriage disintegrate.

'The thing is that I do like to drink. Two glasses of Bagpiper Gold at night is what I look forward to. After the day's work, dealing with incompetent proofreaders, prima donna copyeditors just back from two years of eating the air in Oxford, lying, conniving, paper dealers who supply you with 80 gsm natural shade when you specifically asked for 90 gsm sunshine and demented house-proud authors for whom "stet" is their favourite four-letter word. I liked nothing more than to come home at 6 p.m. and watch Joyce cook the dinner in the kitchen while Portia did her homework at my desk. Dean Martin on the stereo, the volume turned low, and a tall coolly sweating tumbler of whisky and ice by my side to complement that sweet baritone. The problem was that after that one glass, feeling happy and secure in my domesticity, I would start telling them about our Scottish legacy, our home in the Highlands. Our descent from Stirling to the native plains. I would get ***bold–italic*** in my happiness. At the words "native plains" Portia would shut her book and go to her friend's flat on the ground floor and Joyce would burn the egg curry again. They were nationalists I guess. And invariably I, the Scottish traitor, would be left with my whisky. I lost my family because of my sentimentality. But the fact is that I loved being in Delhi, I loved my life. Hell, I am a nationalist too. I drink Bagpiper Gold.'

But when Hriday would point out, 'Crown, you drink every day even now,' Crown would only say 'no comments from the Soviet press. *Tass*', and a tight mask of displeasure would come over his amiable face.

'I think the problem was that they thought my Scottish

legacy was a joke and I made a fool of myself when I drank. Joyce came from solid Bihari-Bengali lower-middle class stock, no one drank in her family. She thought it was sinful and decadent and that one day I would drink them all to penury.'

Hriday would watch Crown at the office and sometimes at home and the utter loneliness of his life would strike him like a hammer. Hriday would realize that family and friends were more important than the artistic life he was striving for. From Crown's despair at the loss of his family and his daily pining for his daughter, Hriday would realize the pain he had caused his own parents by cutting himself off and dropping out of his M.Phil course in Shakespeare Studies. He met his tutor in the M.Phil course and after much pleading got back to his course work. He wouldn't get his room back in Gwyer Hall, of course. A couple of afternoons in the week Hriday would go over to the Arts Faculty building in the North Campus for his lectures and in the evening, work on his thesis. The work on the novel suffered of course but it was needed. He started calling up his parents once every few days and told them that he now had a job again and was also back to doing his M.Phil. He promised them he would complete it this time round and also sit for the NET examination later in the year. At the university he also tracked down his old friends and resumed contact and would meet them for beer and a Mithun Chakraborty movie at Batra on Sunday afternoons like before.

'I realized I didn't want to be self-contained anymore,' Hriday told Imogen. Clouds had gathered overhead and now a cool breeze was blowing in from the east. The oppressive heat of the afternoon had suddenly dissolved.

'To be a writer you do not need to shut yourself off from the world. Look at me, I am halfway across the world from my home, here in the native plains, hustling the East.'

'Ah, dear old Rudyard. Crown would have loved you. He would have taken you under his wing. He would have proofread you to within an inch of your life. You should let me read your manuscript.' Hriday stretched himself out on a nearby tombstone and looked up at the sky. He could smell the rain, gathering steam near Subzi Mandi, off the grass. He was like a dog when it came to rain and women. And yonder still over the Kargil heights, if he would cock his ears a bit northwards, he could hear the proud recoil of the Bofors guns.

'And what are you doing? Hustling the West?'

'Actually, my job. Acquiring.'

Imogen looked at Hriday stretched out, almost at her feet, and realized that this display of laconic familiarity was all for her benefit. The boy was flirting with her and as she thought about it she realized she was responding. And had been responding for some time now. With a tilt to her neck and deeper lilt to her voice. She noticed his thick wrists, the slender bomb-maker fingers and the small cleft on the chin, which emphasized the openness of his smile. Above all she liked his calmness and his frank interest in her.

'What's the title of your work? Not "Tombstone Blues" I hope?'

'No, I haven't decided yet,' Imogen gave a slow smile and said.

'How about "A Fine and Private Place"?'

'Not bad, but none I think do there embrace.'

'Yes, but there could be exceptions,' Hriday smiled back and offered bluntly.

Unlike many Western girls, Imogen actually found Indian men, if they were well brought-up and had good table manners, fairly attractive. She had had a Bangladeshi boyfriend for a while when she was an undergraduate at the University of Newcastle and he had impeccable manners. But Delhi men on the whole she found to be vainglorious and rude. In her three months' sojourn in Delhi, she had gone out with two men, one a Syrian Christian professor of Sociology at JNU and another her regular Sikh taxi driver, who she later found out was married and had three daughters. She stopped travelling by taxis after the first month. Travelling by the Delhi Transport Corporation buses was cheaper and safer, she realized.

With both the men she had gone out just once, sucked in by their good looks and loneliness. Both of them had taken her out to watch *The Lion King* at Chanakya and with both she had the sensation, with all the furtive groping and fondling as soon as the lights were switched off, that she would get profoundly raped before the night was through. She didn't even say goodbye as they dropped her at her flat on Pusa Road. Even though the hopeful Malayali professor had even suggested 'coffee' with twinkling eyes at her doorstep. Just a quick wave of her hand and a loud 'okey dokey' and off she went, without a backward glance. She shifted to the Hotel Kibbutz in Paharganj after the fiasco with the taxi driver. And now in a few weeks' time, her Indian adventure would come to an end, and she would be back in Edinburgh in her tiny attic flat with a view of the Holyrood Palace, taking with her no memories of a travel romance. On the other hand, as she looked speculatively at Hriday, she had the feeling of quite reassurance that many other girls had felt when they met him for the first time. He had a remote quality which spoke of discretion and dark sexual delights and coupled with that scholarly face and head-boy manner, it was frankly disturbing. He could open your bra with two fingers while whispering Andrew fucking Marvell in your ears, Imogen felt. Oh dear.

Samson, the diminutive gravedigger, ambled over and gave Imogen the photostats. She gave him a fifty rupees tip. Samson did a quick impromptu twist like a young Helen and then ran back into the trees.

'I think I should leave now. It is not hot anymore.' Imogen stood up and extended her hand to Hriday.

'Perhaps we can meet again. I could show you the cemeteries in Agra. Also, take in the Taj Mahal by moonlight.'

'Already done that. But yes, let's do meet. I go away at the end of the month.'

'I would love to read your manuscript. Where are you putting up?'

'Hotel Kibbutz, Paharganj. It is fairly well-known.'

'I have seen it. Had apple strudel at the Vedic cafe there once, the Madhuparka. A long time back, a friend of mine, Jai Shankar Sharma, used to live there.'

'He still does. He is the manager, you know. Decidedly odd if you ask me. He offered to wash my track pants once. Paharganj is so ripe with characters. Come over for some strudel and tea on Saturday evening. The honey-glazed holy cow is to die for, by the way. I should be home. And thank you for telling me the story of Samuel Crown.'

'I am going to pick up the Crown jewels now. Would you like to come with me? It is a short walk,' Hriday got up, dusted the dirt and grass off his jeans.

In the five months that Hriday worked with Crown, he learnt more about the nuts and bolts of the publishing business than if he had joined as an editorial assistant in one of the bigger and more glamorous firms. His life had stabilized and he was not drinking hard anymore. He worked diligently at the publishing house and he worked hard for his M.Phil. And then three days back when Hriday received a phone call at Proscenium, around 11.30 from Crown's landlady that Crown was not opening the door and that no one had seen him since yesterday evening, Hriday knew something was terribly wrong. George Tekari asked him to go quickly and take a look. Hriday hailed an autorickshaw from Delhi Gate and was outside Crown's door in fifteen minutes. Mrs Chawla, in her orange and green standard issue Malayali nightie, was standing beside the door. Hriday knocked loudly and called out Crown's name a few times. Mrs Chawla shook her head.

'I am afraid, Mrs Chawla, I will have to kick in the door.' The door gave in at the third try.

'You go in first,' Mrs Chawla said to Hriday. Around that time Dudley Brown arrived from the Maypole Club. Crown was lying unconscious just beyond the choukhat of the door. He was in his white kurta-pyjamas and had crawled from his bedroom to the front door before losing consciousness. Hriday tried reviving him with water and when his eyes fluttered and opened he slipped between his lips a Disprin tablet which he had in his wallet. Hriday had started carrying Disprin tablets since his father's heart attack a few years ago. Crown revived a bit and whispered, 'Portia, do your homework.' Brown ran off to find a taxi.

At LNJP hospital, they confirmed Hriday's diagnosis, Crown had suffered a massive heart attack early in the morning. It was touch and go. He revived in the evening but they kept him in the ICU as they wanted to watch him for the next twenty-four hours. Hriday spent the next afternoon at the hospital with Crown and when George Tekari visited in the evening, Crown gave him Portia's number from his pocket diary but George couldn't get through to Sydney from his cell phone. 'We will try again tomorrow, Sam. Don't you worry. You will be fine in a couple of days. Take a few weeks off. Read Dickens.'

'No, George, I will be back on Monday. I have never taken a break in my life. I am all right. I am still fit.'

'Of course, you are. I will see you tomorrow.' George felt the knot of his tie in an absent-minded manner and walked out of the room, after checking the corridor first for Moscow Centre assassins.

'If I die, Hriday, you can have a selection of my books. The rest can go to the Maypole Club. Dudley can have the stereo and the long playing records. He is a good man. Mrs Chawla can have the rest of my possessions. The bed is hers. Give George the Corona. Here's my Allahabad Bank passbook. Make sure Portia gets everything. She is the nominee.' Hriday was astonished to learn that the account had a little over six lakh rupees in it.

'Crown, you will be fine. Now don't get sentimental on me. I will visit early tomorrow.' Hriday left then as the visiting hours were over and the nurse had knocked twice loudly on the door.

Crown suffered another attack early in the morning and died around 6.30 a.m. When Hriday arrived at around 9.15, he got the news and went up and saw the body. He then came down and called up Tekari and Brown from a phone kiosk run by a paraplegic from his rickshaw outside the front gates of the hospital.

Hriday collected the Crown jewels and a few literary biographies, of Hemingway by Carlos Baker, of Kipling by Carrington and Tolstoy by Troyat. All in the elegant and sturdy Pelican editions from the 1960s. And, of course, *A Suitable Boy*. The rest of the books would go to the Maypole Club. He pointed to the samovar and Imogen Burns picked it up. The solemn Russian women seemed to wave to him, amidst the burning haystacks. They closed the broken door and went upstairs to say goodbye to Mrs Chawla. On the way down Hriday remembered the Corona 3 and picked it up for George.

# Acknowledgements

Thanks to: my parents, brother Sanjay and relatives in Patna and beyond. Shruti Debi, Palash K. Mehrotra, Amitava Kumar, Chandrahas Choudhury, Nisha Susan and Pankaj Mishra. Ramesh Jain and my colleagues at Manohar.

Team Aleph: David Davidar, Ravi Singh, Bena Sareen, Simar Puneet, Aienla Ozukum, P K Sharma, and Meenakshi Singh. Dyuti Mittal for the cover. In the end as always Pragya Sinha Chowdhury.